BURIED TREASURES
OF
NEW ENGLAND

Books in W. C. Jameson's
Buried Treasures series:

BURIED TREASURES OF NEW ENGLAND

*Legends of Hidden Riches,
Forgotten War Loots,
and Lost Ship Treasures*

W.C. Jameson

August House Publishers, Inc.
LITTLE ROCK

Printed in the United States of America

10 9 8 7 6 5 4 3 2 1

LIBRARY OF CONGRESS CATALOGING-IN-PUBLICATION DATA

Buried Treasure of New England / W. C. Jameson.
p.   cm.
Includes bibliographic references.
ISBN 0-87483-485-6 (alk. paper)
1. Treasure-trove—New England. 2. New England—Antiquities.
3. Legends—New England. I. Title.
F6.J36 1997   96-39749
974.4—dc21   CIP

President and publisher: Ted Parkhurst
Executive editor: Liz Parkhurst
Project editor: Suzi Parker
Cover design and maps: Wendell E. Hall

The paper used in this publication meets the minimum requirements
of the American National Standards for Information Sciences—
permanence of Paper for Printed Library Materials, ANSI.48-1984

AUGUST HOUSE, INC.   PUBLISHERS   LITTLE ROCK

Contents

Introduction

Rich in culture, fertile in landscape, and bubbling with legend and lore, New England remains one of the most fascinating regions in the United States. Much of that fascination stems from the impressive tradition of tales and legends of lost mines, buried treasures, hidden fortunes, and chests and ships packed with pirate booty lost and sunk off the sandy coasts.

According to folklore experts, New England, so named by Captain John Smith, rivals the American Southwest and California as the source of some of the nation's most thrilling, compelling, and mysterious cases of lost treasures. While several of these treasures have been discovered, most of them remain lost, and their associated tales and legends have lured treasure hunters, archaeologists, and researchers to the region for more than two centuries. The search continues today.

New England, located in the northeasternmost corner of the United States, consists of Maine, Vermont, New Hampshire, Massachusetts, Rhode Island, and Connecticut. To the north, this region is bordered by Canada. The westward boundary is comprised entirely of the state of New York, which, during early settlement and frontier times, was regarded as a dangerous and forbidding wilderness. To the east and south, New England meets the waters of the Atlantic Ocean.

The Land

New England lies within a portion of a vast geological setting scientists call the Appalachian Provinces. The impressive mountains found in the extreme northeastern states are part of the great Appalachian chain, which dominates much of the eastern part of the country and extends in a general southwest-northeast strike from central Alabama and Georgia into Canada.

The New England province of the Appalachian Mountain range consists primarily of ancient metamorphic rock hundreds of millions of years old, which has been uplifted, folded, and faulted into a variety of shapes and sizes. These exposed rock slopes and surfaces have subsequently been eroded and sculpted into their present configurations and sizes by a variety of natural agents including glaciers, flowing water, and climatic stresses. The principal mountains found in New England are the White and Green Mountains of Vermont and the Hoosac Mountains and Berkshire Hills of western Massachusetts. In the Green Mountains, relief of up to six thousand feet can be found.

During the past one million years, a number of glacial advances and retreats were responsible for the dramatic erosion and deposition of sediment and the subsequent formation of related features such as striae, glacial lakes, erratics, outwash plains, and moraines.

In the recent geologic past of just a few thousand years, climax vegetation communities evolved to cloak the land in a variety of forest cover. Dense and widespread strands of spruce and fir, which cover much of Maine, can be found in the northern part of the region. Northeastern hardwoods dominate most of the central part of New England, and mixed oak and hickory forests are most commonly found throughout the southern portion of the region in Massachusetts, Connecticut, and Rhode Island.

Along the irregularly shaped coastline, a profusion of bays, beaches, sandbars, and spits characterize a narrow zone transitional between the oceans and the interior. The shapes and configurations of many of these coastal features change regularly over the years because of the erosive and depositional potential of storm-driven ocean waters.

The Culture

Much of the nucleus of New England's white settlement in the seventeenth and eighteenth centuries consisted largely of colonists from England. On arriving in America in search of opportunity and a new way of life, these early residents gradually discovered their agricultural technology was poorly suited to the cold and infertile lands they encountered.

This lack of agricultural potential caused many of them to turn to other occupations such as fishing, trading, manufacturing, and lumbering—industries that continue to flourish today. As in virtually all societies, a few who fared poorly at these endeavors turned to outlawry, and New England boasts a history rich in colorful bandits and rogues, as well as pirates who sailed the oceans and occasionally raided coastal communities.

Within a short time of the European migrants' initial arrival, a great variety of ethnic groups resided side by side in New England, including British, Scotch-Irish, Germans, and Swedes. They, in turn, lived alongside a number of different native Indian tribes who had occupied this region for hundreds of years. New England was, indeed, America's first melting pot.

Within this cultural milieu evolved a great deal of interaction in the form of cooperative existence and trade. Not only was the trading of goods and furs commonplace, but the exchange of ideas, notions, and stories became an important aspect of the growing New England communities. The folkways of some ethnic groups were introduced to others who often found them useful in this new land, sometimes even necessary for survival. The sharing of myriad wisdom, food preparation, and medical knowledge throughout the region led to a cultural diffusion and the subsequent adoption of these ways. Through the generations, the individual and collective experiences and adventures of the residents were related and retold in the oral tradition.

In addition to information related to survival and quality of life, various cultures also shared stories, tales, legends, and myths, and in this manner, a number of fascinating and compelling tales of lost mines and buried and hidden treasures contributed by both natives and newcomers grew, becoming a substantial part of the culture.

Treasure Lore

One of the earliest New Englanders to research and record many of the area's fascinating tales of lost treasure was Edward Rowe Snow. In 1951, Snow published *True Tales of Buried Treasure*, an engrossing and well-written book about lost and buried pirate treasure as well as treasures lost and found throughout the entire realm of New England. Snow was a tireless researcher and possessed special feelings for the region and its people.

In 1981, Snow's *Pirates, Shipwrecks, and Historical Chronicles* was published to the delight of his readers and treasure researchers throughout the country. To this day, Snow's works serve as a starting point for most of the subsequent research of New England treasure lore and legend.

As early as the 1970s, I became interested in the study of New England tales and legends of lost and buried treasures and used Snow's *True Tales of Buried Treasure* as an inspiration to pursue the stories in greater detail, poke around in archives, and interview old-timers in an attempt to obtain more information and insight into many of the legends. At the time, a distance of more than two thousand miles separated my home from New England, making intensive study difficult, and, at times, impossible. On the few occasions I did travel to New England, my research was restricted because of scheduling and time constraints, and the amount of study I was able to conduct in libraries revealed precious little information.

Fortunately, I was introduced to Michael Paul Henson, a well-known collector of tales about lost mines and buried treasures. Henson was a prolific writer, and, over the years, he had filled file cabinets with research and observations on tales of treasure from New England as well as much of the rest of the United States. Over several months, Henson provided me with copies of dozens of magazine articles that he had written along with hundreds of pages of handwritten notes on a variety of treasure tales and related topics. Henson's material, along with what I uncovered and accumulated from subsequent research and explorations, filled in many gaps and brought to light several new and exciting tales, which were essentially unknown to the general public. Many of them are presented for the first time in this book.

The fact that millions of dollars' worth of treasure have been lost or buried in New England is an inarguable one; it has been proven time and again over the years. A number of these treasures have been discovered and recovered, but for the most part, they remain lost or hidden, constantly attracting the research attention of treasure hunters, professional and amateur alike.

As the profession of treasure hunting improves with significant advances in technology, and as persistent research uncovers more and more important leads relative to the accurate historical perspective and the real and potential locations of many of these treasures, it is likely that more of them will be uncovered in the future.

Lost or found, these treasures and their tales and legends remain important and captivating elements of the lore of New England.

MAINE

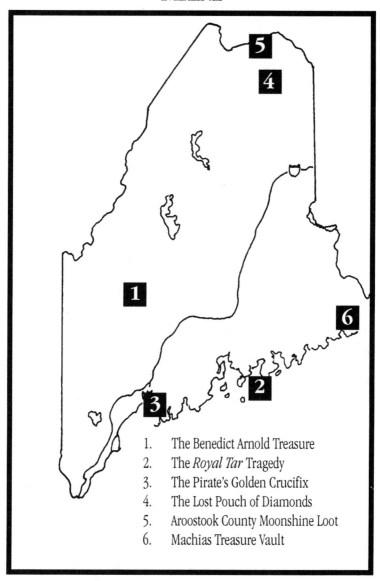

1. The Benedict Arnold Treasure
2. The *Royal Tar* Tragedy
3. The Pirate's Golden Crucifix
4. The Lost Pouch of Diamonds
5. Aroostook County Moonshine Loot
6. Machias Treasure Vault

Machias Treasure Vault

The community of Machias, Maine, is located just inside Machias Bay near the state's eastern end. Today, Machias and nearby Machiasport are regarded by many as tourist destinations, but for many decades, the region served as a hideout for pirates. One of the worst of the sea-going marauders who frequented Machias Bay was Samuel Bellamy, known to friend and foe alike as Black Bellamy. Around 1716, Bellamy selected the narrow, sheltered inlet, where the Machias River entered the bay, as an ideal location to launch raids against coastal communities and merchant ships up and down the Atlantic Coast. The location was easily defensible, and from a nearby vantage point the entire bay could be observed. The Machias Bay hideaway also offered a plentiful supply of fresh water, a deep harbor for ships, and the adjacent woods provided plenty of wild game.

In 1716, Black Bellamy, a fierce pirate, claimed this part of Maine as his own, and with the help of his sailors, along with dozens of captives, constructed a fort at Machias Bay. Here, Bellamy intended to establish a kingdom, where he named himself as ruler for life. From this kingdom, Black Bellamy stated he could command the Atlantic Ocean and the entire East Coast.

Black Bellamy's fort—constructed of thick, heavy logs and surrounded by a deep moat and an earthen wall—was designed so that it could be easily defended. Defense was uppermost in Black Bellamy's mind, for within the log walls of this impressive structure, it is believed that the pirate actually excavated a huge

14

underground vault, where he placed a considerable amount of booty taken during several years of plundering the high seas. With the help of a longtime confederate named Paulsgrave Williams, Bellamy designed and engineered this impressive vault. According to legend, the vault was set at a great depth, lined with flagstone, and roofed with heavy oak beams. Into this secret chamber, the pirate placed chests and bags containing gold and silver bars, coins, weapons, and jewels. At the time, no one knew about the treasure vault save for Black Bellamy and Williams, because once the workers completed the project, they were killed. At today's values, Bellamy's hoard is estimated to be worth between $15 and $35 million.

Believing that a kingdom needed a supply of workers and women, Black Bellamy decided to acquire some. After handpicking a contingent of fighting seamen, he and Williams set out in two sailing vessels in early 1717 southwestward along the coast. Black Bellamy heard that many of the settlements along the Atlantic Coast to the south were filled with able-bodied men and desirable females, and with two shiploads of pirates, he decided to invade the towns, loot the stores, and steal men and women to help populate his Machias kingdom.

Though a veteran of dozens of successful raids, both on shore and sea, Black Bellamy encountered near-disaster on this voyage. Only a few days after leaving Machias, Black Bellamy's ship, the *Widah*, was spotted by the lead vessel of a French escort transporting troops to Quebec. The French ship, which sported twenty-six guns, inflicted serious damage to the two pirate vessels. With both pirate ships leaking badly from several places, Black Bellamy remarkably was able to lead them back to the Machias stronghold for repairs.

In April 1717, Black Bellamy sailed out again in the renovated *Widah*. Undeterred by the possibility of hostile encounter, the pirates plied the coastal waters toward Massachusetts, bent on raiding. Just off Nantucket Island, Black Bellamy attacked and captured the ship *Mary Anne* and looted it of goods and treasure. With the *Widah's* hold now filled with newly acquired riches, Black Bellamy decided to anchor just offshore from the town of New Bedford and launch a raid the following morning.

About two hours before sunrise on April 26, an ocean storm, surging into the region from the southeast, brought heavy rains and violent winds. Unable to withstand the storm's fury, the *Widah* broke apart and quickly sank to the continental shelf's sea bottom, not far from Nantucket Island. Black Bellamy, along with a crew of one hundred and forty three men, disappeared beneath the ocean waves. Much of what is known of the last few hours of the *Widah* was learned from two pirates who managed to swim to shore, and they related that a fortune in gold, silver, and goods went down with the ship.

Weeks later, the inhabitants of Black Bellamy's Machias kingdom received the news of the pirate's death. Many captives, no longer enslaved, walked away. Some constructed crude rafts and set out to sea, while others simply began hiking down the shore along the coast, hoping to reach a port before starving to death.

The few brigands Bellamy left on the island to supervise the affairs of the young kingdom were incapable of leadership or the fort's maintenance, and they eventually drifted off. Within a few weeks, the stronghold overlooking Machias Bay was deserted and never occupied again.

Time passed, and the logs and timbers of the old pirate fortress gradually decomposed returning to the soil. The moat eventually filled in, and the earthworks surrounding the fort eroded into a low semi-circular mound. Trees, shrubs, and grasses grew up in what was once the structure's interior.

As recently as the 1940s, a portion of the earthen wall could still be seen but remains no more. Many claim to know the precise, original location of Black Bellamy's old fort, however, and adventurers arrive in the area on occasion to excavate for the vast treasure vault believed to exist somewhere deep in the ground.

In recent years, some researchers have insisted that Black Bellamy's incredible treasure was not buried inside the fort at all, but rather out in the woods, perhaps as much as fifty yards from the site of the structure. No one can say in which direction from the fort the alleged treasure lies, but most who ascribe to this theory search the area behind the long gone fortress.

Many holes have been excavated in search of Black Bellamy's fabulous treasure cache, but nothing has ever been found. From all accounts, the treasure vault lies at least fifteen feet below the surface, perhaps more, and it is likely that in the past two-and-a-half centuries since Black Bellamy's death the elusive chamber has caved in, maybe leaving a slight depression in the ground.

Sensitive high-tech probing sensors could be capable of locating the underground treasure vault. At this writing, an organization of seven men who have designed and constructed such a device is preparing to apply to the state of Maine for permission to undertake an organized search for Black Bellamy's treasure.

The Benedict Arnold Treasure

Most Americans are aware of Benedict Arnold's reputation as a traitor, but few know that he is also linked to a lost treasure chest filled with gold coins, still lying deep in the heart of the western Maine woods.

During the summer of 1775, Benedict Arnold, then holding the rank of colonel in General George Washington's army, presented a plan to his commander for the invasion and capture of Quebec City. Washington knew that Arnold was familiar with the region because of his numerous expeditions to the area, so the general entrusted him to lead a campaign through the Maine wilderness and to the threshold of the walled fortress. In order for Arnold to pay his troops, employ guides, and purchase supplies and ammunition, Washington provided him with a chest filled with gold coins believed to be worth $54,000 at the time.

Arnold's expedition left Boston Harbor on September 13, 1775, and sailed to Newburyport, New Hampshire. The ships paused only long enough to load troops, supplies, and fresh water. Sometime early in October, the ships landed at the mouth of the Kennebec River near the present-day city of Brunswick, Maine, where the soldiers planned to load themselves and their supplies on rafts and pole up the river until they were to strike out across land. After a close examination of the rafts, however, Arnold declared them useless because most were rotted. Hiring several local woodsmen and carpenters, the colonel ordered the construction of an entirely new fleet of rafts. In order to compensate the

18

workers for their labor, Arnold opened the chest and paid out several gold coins while approximately a dozen soldiers stood nearby and gazed at the great riches in the wooden chest.

The construction of the rafts delayed the trip, and this troubled Arnold. He feared his company of soldiers would arrive at Quebec City too late to be of any use. When the troops finally got underway, Arnold forced them into long days of hard travel in an attempt to reach Quebec City in time to be involved in an effective assault.

The forced journey up the Kennebec River met with one disaster after another. Often the troops were required to pull the rafts through muddy swamps and portage the heavy crafts, along with supplies and cannons, past numerous rapids and waterfalls. Several cannons were lost when the straps securing them to the rafts snapped, tumbling the heavy, ungainly objects into the river.

Because a significant portion of the food supply had been swept into the river, food shortages soon began to have a telling effect on the soldiers. To compound the problem, very little game was found in the surrounding woods. By the end of the second week of October, the men were consuming their shoe leather, suffering from starvation and dysentery, and freezing in the unseasonably low temperatures that descended upon the region. With the prospect of facing even more hardship before reaching Quebec, dozens of troops deserted.

One afternoon as Arnold's personal raft carrying the war chest was negotiating a tricky set of rapids on the Dead River just north of present-day Eustis, the vessel's timbers cracked and separated from their lacings, plunging the heavy gold-filled chest into the torrent. Having neither the time nor the equipment necessary to retrieve the chest, Arnold could do little more than try to reach Quebec City on time.

Finally, on December 13, Arnold's troops, along with the command of General Richard Montgomery, launched an attack on Quebec City. By the time the battle ended, the Americans had suffered a terrible defeat, Montgomery had been killed, and Arnold seriously wounded.

As soon as he was well enough to travel, Arnold returned to General Washington's command and never was able to go back to the Dead River and retrieve the chest of gold coins.

Four years later in Philadelphia, Arnold was asked to account for the $54,000 in gold coins entrusted to him, and it is from his own testimony during that inquisition that we know much of what transpired during the forced march through Maine.

Some researchers contend that Arnold did not lose the gold at all, but instead buried it somewhere along the route with the intention of returning for it later. Whatever the case, numerous eyewitnesses stated that the war chest never was again seen following the negotiation of the rapids on the Dead River.

If Arnold's war chest had, indeed, tumbled into the swirling waters of the Dead River, the heavy gold coins could still be lying at that stream's bottom.

Those who believe Benedict Arnold's chest of gold coins lies buried somewhere near the Dead River rapids also believe it is imminently retrievable. A few who have researched Arnold's testimony believe that to be the case, and in recent years, treasure hunters equipped with sensitive metal detecting devices have been searching this stream's shore in hope of recovering the fortune.

The *Royal Tar* Tragedy

With ceremonial hoopla, the *Royal Tar* was launched in 1835 amid high praise from shipping officials, who claimed the steamship manifested the finest construction of any ship sailing on the Atlantic Ocean. They also stated that the vessel was the safest ship operating in the world.

The *Royal Tar*, a steam-powered side-wheeler, was one hundred and sixty-four feet long and boasted palatial passenger accommodations, rivaling those found in the finest hotels of the day. Primarily regarded as a passenger ship, the *Royal Tar*, which was constructed at the renowned port of St. John, also carried freight during its regular runs along the Maine and New Brunswick coasts.

In mid-October 1836, a circus, which had just completed a successful tour of several Canadian provinces, chartered the *Royal Tar* to carry personnel and equipment back to the United States. To accommodate the people, equipment, and animals aboard the ship, it was necessary to remove a number of lifeboats to make room.

Heavy with the circus freight, animals, employees, administrators, and the normal contingent of passengers and cargo, the *Royal Tar* rode dangerously low in the water as it steamed out of St. John Harbor. Because the animal cages were placed on the ship's decks, efficient movement from one end of the vessel to the other was inhibited, and the extremely crowded conditions kept most of the passengers in their rooms. In spite of the overload, the

Royal Tar entered a relatively calm sea and performed admirably on its way to its charted destination—Portland, Maine.

As was the custom on ocean voyages like this one, passengers who carried large amounts of money and other valuables requested they be placed in the ship's safe. It is estimated that between $35,000 and $50,000 worth of gold and silver coins, along with several pieces of fine expensive jewelry, were locked securely in the safe.

A scheduled stop for the *Royal Tar* was Vinalhaven, a small town located on the island with the same name at the mouth of Penobscot Bay. The *Royal Tar* would drop anchor for a day and night while supplies were replenished.

As a number of officers and crew went ashore to arrange for deliveries, a storm approached from the southeast out in the Atlantic. Though passengers and crewmen alike expressed concern that the increasingly high winds and heavy seas might cause problems with the overloaded ship, James Reed, the ship's captain, assured them that the *Royal Tar* was built to endure such things. Little did Reed know that as he visited with passengers and crew in the dining hall, a completely unforeseen disaster was unfolding in the boiler room.

Though the *Royal Tar* was solidly constructed with the finest and strongest materials, a great deal of the machinery used to power the vessel did not meet such rigid standards. One of the huge boilers proved defective, and as a result, some of the planking adjacent to it caught fire. In a very short time, the flames spread throughout the boiler room and surrounding sections and onto the decks where they were fanned by the high winds from the growing storm. Within minutes, the fire blazed out of control, and evacuation attempts were underway.

Because of the crowded conditions aboard the *Royal Tar* along with the reduced number of lifeboats, evacuation proved difficult and dangerous. As the burning ship rocked in the waves of the choppy ocean, Captain Reed spotted the arrival of a government cutter, which hove to about fifty yards away. When Reed motioned for the cutter to come closer to aid the rescue, the captain of the smaller boat informed him that it was carrying a quantity of gunpowder and he feared an explosion.

Boarding a lifeboat, Captain Reed was rowed to the cutter where he assumed command, piloted the vessel to a relatively safe position near the *Royal Tar*, and managed to save many lives. All of the circus equipment, along with the animals, were left on board.

Approximately four hours later, the burned *Royal Tar* slowly sank into the sea just off Vinalhaven Island. It was only then that Captain Reed realized that the retrieval of the ship's safe had been forgotten during the rescue attempts.

Several months later, a salvage company, commissioned by the organization responsible for the *Royal Tar*'s funding and construction, spent several weeks off the coast of Vinalhaven Island working to retrieve a number of items from the sunken vessel, including the ship's safe. Choppy seas and high winds jeopardized the salvage attempts from the first day, and after two weeks the company finally left the area, having found nothing of value. A second attempt to locate and retrieve the safe of the *Royal Tar* funded by the same Canadian organization also met with failure.

During the 1850s, two independent salvage companies probed the sunken wreckage of the *Royal Tar* but were unable to find the safe.

In 1930, a New York City salvage team spent a week in the waters off Vinalhaven Island searching for the safe. According to the divers, the *Royal Tar* had broken up, probably as a result of storm-generated turbulence, and its remains were scattered for hundreds of yards across the ocean floor. In addition, bottom sands had covered much of the wreckage. The safe was never found.

In 1953, research was undertaken preparing for yet another attempt to find the safe of the *Royal Tar*. This time, however, the salvage crew was unsuccessful in locating any of the wreckage.

No further attempts to retrieve the safe of the *Royal Tar* have been recorded, and it is believed that it still lies just off the coast of Vinalhaven Island in the sands of the deep Penobscot Bay near where it joins the Atlantic Ocean. If recovered today, the gold and silver coins, along with the jewelry, would be worth $1 million.

The Pirate's Golden Crucifix

Pirate Captain Bartholomew Roberts was one of the most unusual plunderers ever to sail the high seas. Always impeccably dressed in a starched shirt with frilled cuffs and a long-tailed black coat, Roberts commanded a ship that was manned by some of the world's most bloodthirsty pirates. In contrast, Captain Roberts never drank liquor, consorted with women, gambled, or spoke coarse words. Though his efforts met with little success, he often cautioned his crewmen about such excesses and tried to get them to follow his example. Roberts even arranged for church services to be held every Sunday aboard ship, but they were seldom attended by anyone other than himself.

In spite of his odd tendency toward immaculate dress and righteousness, Roberts was known as a vicious fighter, a completely fearless leader, and has been credited with capturing and sinking more than four hundred ships and the killing of more than a thousand men.

Before a raid, Roberts had his personal barber cut his hair and manicure his nails. Following this, the pirate captain dressed himself in clean, freshly pressed garments and polished boots. Around his neck, he hung his prized possession—a large heavy golden crucifix studded with a dozen large diamonds. The cross—believed to have once resided in a Catholic mission in Mexico—was taken during the raid of a Spanish galleon months earlier.

On the morning of February 10, 1722, while sailing from a small island stronghold in the West Indies, Roberts's vessel was approached by the *Swallow*, a heavily armed British warship. Captain Chaloner Ogle, a highly decorated officer who commanded the *Swallow*, had been given the responsibility of capturing or killing Roberts, a troublesome pirate who was responsible for the disruption of important trade between England and the Americas as well as the sinking of numerous British ships.

As the *Swallow* approached the pirate ship, Roberts, as was his custom, dressed in his finest clothes, hung the golden crucifix around his neck, and went out onto the deck just as the British ship fired its cannons.

For nearly an hour the two ships exchanged cannon fire, but the pirate vessel received the worst from the encounter. One well-placed shot from the *Swallow* struck a mast near where Roberts stood on deck, and a piece of shattered wood from the explosion pierced Roberts's throat. Bleeding heavily, the pirate leader, unnoticed by his fighting crewmen, fell to the deck. Within minutes Roberts, the scourge of the Atlantic and Caribbean, was dead.

Nearly every week at sea, Roberts reminded his crewmen that if he ever fell in battle, they were to throw his body into the sea. Following his wishes, several of the pirates, on noticing their fallen leader, picked him up and were about to throw him overboard when First Mate Richard Kennedy came forward and yanked the golden crucifix from his dead captain's neck. While the battle between the two ships still raged, Kennedy raced below deck and hid the crucifix among his belongings.

A short time later, it became apparent that the pirate vessel was losing the battle and would soon be defeated. Sailors and crewmen began throwing up their hands in surrender, hoping they would be spared execution. Finally, the *Swallow* tied onto the pirate ship, and British sailors swarmed the conquered vessel to chain the captured brigands.

First Mate Kennedy, on being shackled, demanded an audience with the commander of the victorious ship, and that evening he was escorted into Ogle's chambers.

Kennedy informed Ogle that he had been present during the burial of numerous treasure-filled chests at locations in the Caribbean that contained tens of thousands of gold coins, jewelry, and precious stones from Roberts's raids on British vessels. If an appropriate arrangement could be made, suggested Kennedy, he would lead Ogle to these treasures. Ogle manifested interest in Kennedy's offer, and the two men discussed the matter well into the night.

Within the week, the captured pirates, along with Kennedy, were taken to a British garrison on a West Indies island and imprisoned while preparations for a trial got under way. During the following month, each pirate was tried, convicted, and hanged—all but Richard Kennedy.

Late one evening, Kennedy was taken from his prison cell and brought before several men, including Ogle. If the prisoner would direct the retrieval of Roberts's buried chests, Ogle told him, the British government would grant him his freedom along with fifteen percent of the value of the recovered treasure.

Kennedy agreed to the proposition, and within weeks a number of coin- and jewelry-filled chests were dug up from various beach locations in the Caribbean Sea. When the recoveries were completed, Kennedy found himself in possession of a fortune, which he packed into four heavy chests with metal fittings. Amazingly, Kennedy had maintained possession of the golden crucifix during his imprisonment, and he placed the valuable object into one of the chests.

With some of his new wealth, Kennedy purchased a light, maneuverable sloop, loaded his four chests into it, and sailed along the Atlantic Coast in search of place to settle. His recent experience with imprisonment, along with the hanging of his companions, convinced him to retire from piracy.

Several weeks later, Kennedy arrived at Boothbay, Maine, decided he liked the area, and moved into an abandoned rock house located far out on the peninsula. For several days thereafter, Kennedy searched throughout the region for a suitable location to bury his treasure. Eventually, he sailed to a portion of the Kennebec River, discovered a remote site that appealed to him, and, after removing enough money to live on for several years, he buried his four chests on a tree-lined hill overlooking the wide stream. The excavation was nearly four feet deep, and after placing the chests into it, he laid two large, flat stones in the hole before filling it. Peeling a piece of birch bark from a nearby tree, Kennedy, using his knife, etched a simple map showing the location of his buried treasure. Satisfied, he returned to his Boothbay home.

Days later, Kennedy obtained a finely tanned calf skin, cut a square from it measuring eighteen inches to each side, and onto this he recreated the map. After carefully recording distances, directions, and landmarks, he placed a star at the site of his buried treasure. Kennedy rolled the map and stored it in his sea chest.

Several months passed, and boredom soon overtook Kennedy in his new location. In spite of his capture and close brush with execution, the pirate found himself longing once again for a high seas adventure. For a time, he considered procuring a suitable ship and seasoned crew and returning to piracy, but ultimately decided against it when he learned that British warships were patrolling the coastal waters in increasing numbers. Instead, Kennedy sailed back to England and purchased a London tavern. In a very short time, he turned the tavern into a brothel, and before the year was out, it had gained a reputation as a hangout for thieves, cutthroats, and pirates. In time, Kennedy's place of business became an informal meeting place for gangs of criminals and freebooters, planning and organizing dozens of robberies and murders.

One evening while very drunk, Kennedy beat one of the prostitutes senseless for spilling a drink on him. The woman vowed revenge and immediately fled to the authorities to report the goings-on at the tavern. For the next few weeks, law enforcement officials watched from hiding as well-known pirates and murderers entered and left the tavern. Determined to shut the notorious establishment down once and for all, they eventually raided it and arrested Kennedy along with several of his henchmen. Kennedy was charged with conspiring to rob and kill a government official—a hanging offense. The former pirate was tried, convicted, and executed within three weeks.

Kennedy's belongings fell into the possession of a pirate named Booth who worked for him. After examining the sea chest's contents, Booth retrieved everything of value and left the rest. He briefly examined the tightly rolled calfskin but could not make sense of Kennedy's cryptic markings and notations. Deciding it was worthless, he threw the skin back into the chest and closed it. Days later, Booth gave the chest to a relative.

The sea chest, containing Richard Kennedy's treasure map and other artifacts, was handed down in the family during successive generations. In 1878, one of the descendants, Terrence Booth, spotted the chest in a storeroom, opened it, and found the calfskin map. The descendant recognized the item for what it was—a treasure map—and determined to find Kennedy's buried cache.

In 1879, the new owner of the map, after setting aside an amount of money, sailed to Maine. The few items he brought with him were packed into the sea chest along with the map. By the time Terrence Booth arrived on the American coast, he had exhausted what little savings he possessed and was forced to find work. For a year, he labored as a hatter's apprentice in Portland until finally saving enough money to continue his search.

Uncertain which of the many rivers that flowed into the Atlantic Ocean was the one identified on Kennedy's map, Booth often became lost. After weeks of sailing and hiking along the coast, he ran short of funds and was again forced to find employment. Finally, in 1882, he grew discouraged and decided to abandon his quest.

One day, Booth learned that a timber company located in Vermont was hiring workers. Desperately short of money with no prospects for employment in the immediate area, he undertook the journey to the logging camp. He grew weary of transporting the sea chest along the way and looked for a place to store it. Late one October afternoon, Booth came to Emeline Benner Lewis's home, a fine house located a short distance from the main road. He knocked on the door, introduced himself, and asked if he could leave his chest with her until he returned. Mrs. Lewis agreed, and after she was paid a small sum, she allowed Booth to place it in the attic. The stranger never returned.

Emeline Lewis's nephew, George Benner, frequently visited her house, and he often inquired about the strange trunk stored in the attic. With the typical curiosity of a young boy, he was desperate to learn what was in it. Mrs. Lewis, however, forbade him to open it because it belonged to someone who promised to come back for it.

By 1900, Mrs. Lewis was convinced that the young man who left the sea chest was not going to return, so she granted Benner, now in his twenties, permission to open it. In the trunk were several letters, one dated 1830, a quadrant, a few sea shells, and the rolled calfskin. From the moment he unrolled it, Benner was fascinated with the map and spent hours each day pouring over it and trying to decipher some of the markings. Benner, who was familiar with the configuration of a portion of Maine's coastline, eventually recognized Casco Bay, Boothbay Harbor, and the mouth of the Kennebec River on the map. At one point along the river was a star, and in one corner of the skin was the inscription:

STAND ABREST QURTSBOLDER
BRING TOP IN LINE WITH HILL N 1/2M
IT LISE 12 FATHOM N.E.
NEAR BIG TREES UNDER STONE

About two months later, Benner, along with a companion that he persuaded to become involved in the project, rented a boat at Boothbay early one morning and sailed up the Kennebec River. After several hours, they arrived at a large granite boulder glistening with quartz crystals. Believing this was the boulder alluded to in the map inscription, Benner and his friend beached the boat and explored the area for two hours.

About one-half mile north of the boulder, they found a low hill with only a single tree growing on it. Closer examination, however, revealed the partially buried trunks of other trees that had apparently flourished on the hill sometime in the past but had eventually succumbed to old age. By the time Benner and his friend determined that this was likely the hill where the treasure was buried, the sun was low on the western horizon. The two men sailed back to Boothbay, purchased some supplies, planning to return early in the morning and resume their search.

Arriving shortly after dawn on the following day, the two returned to the low hill carrying a long metal bar, two shovels, and a number of canvas sacks. With the bar, they probed the ground, stabbing it into the soft sand every few feet. Finally, they encountered rock-like resistance about two feet beneath the surface near a very old tree stump.

Another twenty minutes of excited digging revealed a large, flat rock lying horizontally. After considerable effort, the two men tilted the rock onto its side only to discover another one beneath it.

The partially caved-in top of a wooden trunk lay directly underneath the second stone. After pulling away the pieces of rotted wood, the two men were nearly speechless when they discovered hundreds of coins before them. One after the other, they filled the canvas sacks with the gold coins. More digging adjacent to this excavation revealed yet another chest and more gold coins. In the second chest, Benner found a golden crucifix containing twelve sparkling diamonds!

After another two hours of removing the coins and placing them in canvas bags, Benner and his companion excavated two more exploratory holes in the area but encountered nothing. Convinced they had located the entire treasure, the two men loaded their newly found wealth, along with the map and tools, into their boat and departed.

They had no way of knowing that, lying within inches of one of their excavations, were two more wooden chests, containing a king's ransom in gold coins.

In the years that followed Benner's discovery, the topography in the valley of the Kennebec River has been dramatically modified as a result of numerous floods and expanding human settlement. The granite boulder described by Kennedy and found by Benner is no longer there, but a number of low hills rise beyond the river banks.

At the top of one of these hills, as far as anyone knows, still lie two of pirate Kennedy's gold-filled treasure chests.

The Lost Pouch of Diamonds

Ever since an international boundary has existed between the United States and Canada, smuggling has been a viable and profitable enterprise. Throughout history, the movement of weapons, trade goods, money, gold, silver, jewels, and government secrets back and forth between Canada and the U.S. has been documented well. Heavy smuggling traffic, particularly during the nineteenth century, often occurred on a number of roads and trails winding through several New England states.

For most of the 1850s, a large smuggling ring actively and successively transported a variety of contraband into the United States from Canada. The cargo, which ranged from arms to gold, was unloaded from ships anchored in Canada's St. Lawrence River or at the docks in Quebec. Packed onto horses and mules, the goods—sometimes stolen, sometimes previously arranged for—were transported through the deep, dense forests into Maine where they were subsequently delivered and distributed.

During this time, Barry Thomas contracted as a carrier for a large Canadian smuggling organization. Thomas, who owned several horses, was paid handsomely to transport contraband from Canada into the United States, ultimately delivering it to receivers at selected destination points, generally along the Atlantic Coast.

Thomas previously worked as a farmer, a logger, and a dockhand, but when he learned that smuggling paid so much more than laboring in the fields, the woods, and in the ports, he turned to a life of crime with few regrets. A widower, Thomas took his only child, a young daughter, along on his smuggling expeditions.

Thomas's daughter, thirteen years old, was a sickly child, and had been in ill health since her birth. In spite of her poor physical condition, Thomas carried her along everywhere he went and saw to her comfort as best he could.

In the summer of 1855, Thomas met clandestinely with a number of smuggling operatives on the St. Lawrence River shore near the Quebec city of Riviere-du-Loup. Here, several bundles and packs of contraband were strapped onto Thomas's pack horses, all of it intended for delivery to Rockland, Maine, where it was to be loaded aboard a British freighter anchored far out in the bay and shipped to New York.

After the heavy parcels had been tied securely, the leader of the smugglers called Thomas aside and handed him a leather pouch. Inside the pouch, he told Thomas, was $200,000 worth of diamonds that were to be delivered personally to a man in Portland, Maine. The man, said the smuggler, would pay a large sum of money upon delivery. Thomas agreed to carry the parcel to Portland, and about an hour later, after loading his daughter onto one of the horses, led the heavily laden pack train from the river and into the woods toward Maine.

Shortly after locating the trail that would take Thomas safely into Maine, it began to rain. Long before noon, the trail grew slick, muddy, and extremely difficult to negotiate. As Thomas led his weary mounts along, he heard his daughter's incessant coughing and feared the foul weather would harm her.

The storm slowed travel considerably, and ten days later the smuggler had only covered one hundred miles. Tired from the long and difficult journey, growing frustrated with the constant downpours, and deeply concerned about his daughter's health, Thomas began to cast about for a place to rest for a few days.

Thomas's route had taken him along the eastern side of Portage Lake, located near the present-day town of Portage, Maine. As he rode southward along the trail, he could see the shining lake below him. To his right, he spotted the relatively gentle slope of Carpenter Ridge, and near the top he saw a dense cluster of trees. Here, he thought, he could find some temporary shelter from the continuous rain and properly care for his sick daughter.

Just over one-half mile from the trail, Thomas found a suitable campsite. After setting his daughter against the protective bole of a large tree and covering her with a heavy coat, he constructed a lean-to from fallen boughs and branches. Following this, he moved her into the crude shelter, built a small fire, and prepared the first hot meal they had eaten in over a week.

During the night, the girl's coughing grew worse and she began having difficulty breathing. Holding her close to keep her warm, Thomas comforted the girl as best he could.

Just before dawn, the rain stopped. As Thomas gently laid his daughter aside to rekindle the small fire, he saw that she was dead. Overcome with grief, Thomas walked into the woods atop the ridge and cried for hours.

He returned to the shelter and sat with her body. A number of emotions swept over him, and he began to blame himself for what happened. Somehow convinced that his daughter's death was a punishment for his criminal activities, Thomas determined on the spot to quit, travel to another part of the country where he was not known, and lead an honest life.

As the clouds passed and the sun warmed and dried the ridge top, Thomas untied all of the bundles from the pack horses and scattered the contraband along the ridge. He then turned all of the horses loose except one.

Not far from the lean-to, Thomas excavated a shallow grave for his daughter, and, after placing her in the cavity, he laid a few wildflowers in her hands. Just before replacing the dirt, Thomas remembered the diamonds he carried. Removing the pouch from his coat pocket, he threw them into the grave.

When he had filled the hole, Thomas smoothed it over and covered it with rocks and broken limbs so that it would appear like any other part of the ridge. After saying a final prayer, Thomas mounted his horse and rode away.

For several years, Barry Thomas worked a variety of jobs—painter, porter, carpenter along the Maine coast. In the days following his daughter's burial, he had taken to drinking and eventually spent most of his pay on whiskey and ale. As a result of his chronic drunkenness, Thomas had difficulty holding down a job and was fired from each one.

In the summer of 1861, Thomas worked as a painter in Portsmouth, New Hampshire. One day he arrived at his place of employment quite drunk and was immediately let go. Destitute, and with no hope of finding work, Thomas decided to return to Carpenter Ridge near Portage Lake and dig up the pouch of diamonds that he had buried six years earlier.

It was nearly a year later when Thomas finally arrived at Portage. Little had changed since the last time he passed this way, and as his route took him along the trail toward Carpenter Ridge, his heart raced while he recalled his last experience here. Climbing the ridge, he felt waves of panic and fear as he approached the resting place of his dead daughter.

Once atop the ridge, Thomas became somewhat disoriented. Though he found some of the contraband he had scattered throughout the area on his previous trip, he was unable to relocate the site of the lean-to. And he could not find his daughter's grave.

With a steadily growing dread, Thomas raced across the contours of the ridge searching for the gravesite. He looked under every log and rock and dug several holes after he thought he had found the correct location, but it was all for naught. By nightfall, Barry Thomas was collapsed against a rock outcrop, sobbing.

The following morning, Thomas walked down from the ridge, followed the trail southward, and eventually arrived at a relative's home near the little settlement of Chesterton on the Penobscot River. Thomas remained with the relative for several days, eating little and growing more and more despondent.

While visiting in Chesterton, Thomas told the relative about his daughter's death and the subsequent burial of the pouch of diamonds. As best he could, Thomas described the ridge and how effectively he had hidden the gravesite. After explaining that he believed he was doomed never to retrieve the diamonds, Barry Thomas walked away and into oblivion. He was never heard from again.

One year later, the relative traveled to Carpenter Ridge to try and locate the diamonds. He found the area much as Thomas had described it and even saw some of the old contraband. Though he searched for several days, he was never able to find anything that remotely resembled a grave.

In 1931, two young boys were playing atop Carpenter Ridge when one of them made a startling discovery. Poking out of the ground near the top of a gentle slope were several bones. After the youngsters related the find to their parents, a small group of area residents was assembled to go to the ridge and investigate.

Sure enough, a cluster of bones lay in what appeared to be a grave, and a brief examination of the bones indicated that they belonged to a child. The investigators cast about for a marker but did not find one.

Disturbing the gravesite as little as possible, the residents carefully set the bones back into it, filled it in, and left. In time, the mysterious little grave's location was forgotten.

Could the lonely grave discovered in 1931 have belonged to Barry Thomas's daughter? It seems likely. If true, just a few more minutes of digging around in the dirt near the young girl's final resting place might well have yielded the pouch of diamonds, established to be worth well over $1 million today, which were left behind by Barry Thomas seventy-six years earlier.

Aroostook County Moonshine Loot

For more than two hundred years, the dense pine forests of Maine have yielded millions of logs to the timber industry. Long before the invention of chain saws, tractors, and other power equipment, the cutting and hauling of trees were accomplished by strong men using saws, axes, and teams of horses and oxen. Often located far from towns, loggers lived for weeks, sometimes months, at a time deep in the woods and close to their work.

Around 1900, an enterprising ne'er-do-well named Anse Handley decided he could make an impressive profit by selling liquor to Maine loggers, and over the years it is believed he pocketed as much as $100,000, most of which was converted to gold. Handley, a notoriously frugal man, buried his fortune in the woods not far from his squatter shack near the Canadian border.

Anse Handley lived most of his adult life moving from place to place around Maine with his wife and two daughters. Handley's moves were seldom initiated by him; more often than not he was simply chased out of an area for one or more criminal activities.

For one thing, Handley was a squatter, and he would often settle on someone else's property, build a crude shack or cabin, hunt local game, and fish the streams. When discovered by the property owner, Handley was generally sent on his way, usually at gunpoint.

Handley also had a reputation as a thief, and many a chicken house located near one of his temporary dwellings was raided, many a cow or pig stolen, and sometimes area homes broken into.

Often caught with his stolen goods, Handley narrowly escaped hanging on several occasions only by quickly throwing his few poor belongings into his rickety wagon and fleeing in the night to friendlier places where he wasn't known.

Handley's wanderings eventually took him into northern Maine near the Canadian border. During the early part of the twentieth century, much of this part of the state was only sparsely settled, and the few opportunities for earning a livelihood were normally associated with timber companies or trapping area streams for beaver and other fur-bearing animals.

The region's remoteness appealed to Handley, and he decided to stay. Moving onto some property owned by a local timber company not far from Fort Kent, a frontier settlement, Handley felled some trees and constructed a crude cabin.

On his first visit to the tiny community of Fort Kent, Handley quickly distinguished himself as a troublemaker. In need of supplies but possessing only a pocketful of change, he haggled and argued with storekeepers until he was thrown out of several establishments.

Handley spent very little time bathing or grooming, and his filthy and unkempt appearance further marked him as a tramp. When Handley finally drove his wagon out of Fort Kent, some store owners noticed items missing from their shelves.

Handley went to work for one of the lumber companies but quit after one week. He cared little for hard labor. But during the time he was sawing and chopping the great pines that grew in the region, Hardley learned that the men who worked in the lumber camps had little or no diversion on nights and weekends. What they wanted more than anything else, they told Handley, were whiskey and women.

Deciding a huge profit could be made from supplying both of these commodities to the lumbermen, Handley went into business for himself.

Several weeks later, Handley arrived at the lumber camp in his horse-drawn wagon around midnight. After surreptitiously making his way through the camp, he entered the big log structure where the loggers ate and slept and informed them he had brought a quantity of fine whiskey for sale as well as two comely women from Fort Kent. For the next four hours, Handley poured moonshine from the crocks in the back of his wagon and assigned each of the women to a succession of the highest bidders. By the time he drove away from the logging camp, his pockets were heavy with coins.

For the next few days, Anse Handley remained busy making moonshine whiskey in the woods not far from his cabin. From time to time, he rode into Fort Kent to recruit a few enterprising young ladies who had no qualms about entertaining the loggers for a price.

Every two or three weeks, Handley, with his wagon loaded down with liquor and women, arrived at the logging camp about two hours past sundown. His business was so successful that he expanded his trade and made visits to other camps in the area. When he was not peddling his wares, he stayed busy enlarging his moonshine still. Handley's wife and daughters helped him make the whiskey.

The owners of the timber companies were angered when they discovered their employees were getting drunk several times each month on bootleg liquor. For a day or two following Handley's visits, productivity slowed considerably as the loggers nursed headaches and staggered about their work half-asleep. Eventually, the owners decided to do something about the problem and hired armed guards to keep the whiskey peddler from coming into the camps.

The presence of the guards proved to be only a minor problem for Handley. In some instances, it was simply a matter of bribing the guards with a gift of whiskey or a few minutes with one of the women. On other occasions, Handley merely snuck into camp from another direction. Sometimes the moonshiner arranged for the loggers to sneak away from the camp and meet him at a predetermined location in the woods where they would enjoy whiskey and women.

In the two-and-a-half years that Anse Handley operated his bootleg liquor and prostitution enterprise, it was estimated that he made between $60,000 and $100,000 dollars in profit. During this time, Handley carried his earnings into Fort Kent and converted them into gold, which he carried back to his squatter cabin. The merchants and bankers in Fort Kent remained puzzled over the relatively large amounts of money Handley brought in, but they could do little about it.

On returning from town to his cabin deep in the woods, Handley carried the gold coins to a secret location and buried them with others. In spite of his growing wealth, Handley spent very little of his money, and he and his family continued to live like beggars. Despite pleas from his wife, he refused to reveal the location of his coin cache. Instead, he promised her that one day when he decided he had accumulated enough gold, they would dig it up and move to Bangor where they would purchase a fine home, expensive clothes, and a new carriage and team.

As the sale of liquor in the logging camps continued, the owners grew more and more concerned and frustrated about the disruptions it caused. Unsuccessful at halting the sale of the moonshine, they searched for other ways to deal with the problem. Eventually, one guard came forth with the information that the whiskey was sold by a man named Anse Handley who was squatting with his family on land owned by one of the timber companies.

One morning at dawn, a group of eight heavily armed timber company guards, accompanied by two owners, arrived at Handley's cabin. Rousting the family from their sleep, the guards ordered them outside. After informing Handley that he was squatting illegally on private property, one of the owners gave the family one hour to load their belongings into the wagon and leave the county. When the prescribed time had passed, Handley's cabin was set afire. As several of the men watched the structure burn to the ground, another guard came out of the woods and announced he had found a still. Using axes and mauls, three men destroyed the kettles, jugs, and tubing.

Handley begged the men to allow him to remain in the area for one more day. Instead, they forced him into his wagon at gunpoint and stood watching as he rode away. Two of the guards were assigned to follow Handley to make certain he remained on the trail and on his way out of the county.

Handley, aware he was being followed, traveled slowly and only covered a few miles before dusk. Around sundown, he pulled off the road to set up camp in a small clearing. The two guards who were following him likewise halted about one hundred yards behind him and remained in the area until they were certain the family was bedded down for the night. Then, they mounted up and rode back to the lumber camp, fully convinced Handley was leaving the county.

After the guards reported in, their supervisor was not so certain Handley would not return and told the two men to maintain a watch near the burned cabin.

The next morning, Handley noted that his trackers had departed. Following breakfast, he loaded the wagon and rode back in the direction from which he had just come. He was determined to return to the site of his former dwelling and retrieve the fortune in gold coins he had buried nearby.

Handley encountered no one along the trail during the trip back. On arriving at the still smoldering cabin, he pulled a shovel from the back of the wagon and turned to walk out into the woods when the two riders from the previous day approached. With drawn pistols, they ordered Handley back into his wagon. He refused.

Standing his ground, Handley told the guards he wasn't leaving until he retrieved some of his belongings. The guards, completely unaware of the existence of Handley's coin cache, warned him once again to climb into his wagon and ride away. In response, Handley cursed them and turned away to walk into the woods.

The two riders guided their mounts to a position in front of the moonshiner and issued yet another warning. Suddenly, Handley raised his shovel and struck the nearest horse across the head, causing it to rear, buck, and throw its rider. When Handley turned toward the second horse and rider, the guard leveled his pistol at his attacker and shot him in the chest. Handley staggered backward several steps, but, raising the shovel, he advanced once again. A second shot caught Handley in the neck and he went down. Screaming for mercy, Handley's wife ran to his lifeless body and threw herself upon her dead husband. With tears in her eyes, she explained to the guard that Handley only wanted to dig up his chest of gold coins.

Surprised at this information, the guard, now joined by his companion, asked Handley's widow to show them where the gold was buried. She told them she never knew.

After loading Handley's body into the wagon, the two guards watched as the sobbing widow and two daughters rode away down the trail.

Excited about the prospect of locating a buried treasure, the two guards walked into the woods in the direction in which Handley was headed before he was shot. Though they searched the area for about two hours, they could not find anything that resembled a likely location for hiding money.

After returning to the lumber company headquarters, the two guards reported to the owner all that had transpired at Handley's cabin. They also told him about the widow's declaration of a buried coin cache. Within minutes, the owner organized a crew of workers and all rode back to the squatter's site. For nearly a full day, they searched the nearby woods for some sign of a likely cache site, but found nothing.

Almost three months later, three men from Waterville, Maine, arrived at the lumber camp asking for directions to Handley's old cabin. When the owner asked what possible interest they could have in the site, they told an amazing story.

According to the newcomers, Handley's widow and two daughters arrived in Waterville where their wagon broke down. One of the men volunteered to repair the vehicle, and his wife invited the tired travelers to their home for a night's lodging and meals. During dinner that night, Handley's widow told her generous hosts about being evicted from the cabin and her husband's murder. She also related that she believed Handley had buried somewhere between $60,000 and $100,000 in gold coins in the woods not far from the cabin.

Intrigued, the host asked directions to the site and told the widow he was interested in searching for the treasure. He told her that if he found it, he would provide her with a generous share. She agreed to the proposition and drew a map for him. Days later, the man, along with two companions, departed for Fort Kent.

Accompanied by the owner of the lumber company, the three Waterville residents rode to Handley's former residence. From the ruined cabin, they noted several narrow trails winding out into the forest in different directions. One by one, they followed each of the paths for nearly a quarter of a mile, searching carefully for potential hiding places along the way. They found nothing.

For nearly a week, the three men camped near the burned cabin and spent their days exploring the woods for some sign of the cache, but in the end they returned to Waterville empty-handed.

The site of Handley's cabin is believed to be northwest of the town of Fort Kent and within sight of the Allagash River. Though the remains of the moonshiner's burnt cabin have rotted away and the actual location may be indeterminable, some pieces of the old still may still be around. With advanced metal detection equipment, Handley's buried fortune stands an excellent chance of being found.

VERMONT

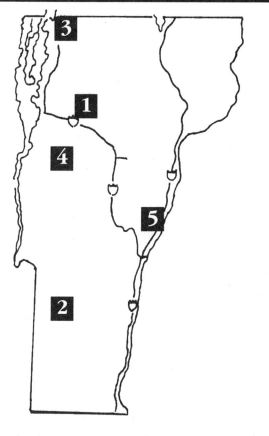

The Ship Mast Magnet's Treasure

For almost twenty years during the 1730s and 1740s, a logger who made his fortune in cutting and selling timber for ship masts regularly buried gold coins near his Vermont cabin. For more than two hundred years following his death, treasure hunters have searched for this fortune in coins, but to date, according to researchers, it has never been found.

During the era of sailing ships, ship builders thought the finest mast timber was found in the forests of Vermont. The mast, or spar, rose vertically from the deck of a ship and supported the yards, booms, and rigging. The mast needed to be straight and strong, and some ships required several of them.

When David Jarvis realized the growing demand for quality masts during the shipbuilding boom of the early 1700s, he decided to go into business providing the finest—a tall, strong, slender, straight pine that grew in central Vermont. Jarvis hired a team of loggers and led them to a site near the upper reaches of the Winooski River, not far from the present-day town of Middlesex. While the loggers cut and trimmed the poles, Jarvis marketed the Vermont masts to shipbuilders along the Atlantic Coast and in Canada. As many as three cut masts were loaded onto large sleds that were pulled by oxen to New Hampshire's Merrimack River. Then, they were lashed together and rafted to the port of Salisbury, Boston, and other important shipbuilding centers. Occasionally, logs were hauled west to Lake Champlain and then northward to the St. Lawrence River.

Before long, Jarvis's fine masts were the talk of the shipbuilding industry. For the builders, as well as for the captains of the vessels, no other mast would do, and the entrepreneur soon had orders for as many poles as he could deliver.

Jarvis required only one thing from those who purchased his masts—they had to pay in gold. During the nearly twenty years that Jarvis operated his mast-cutting business, it is estimated that he accumulated thousands of dollars' worth of gold coins. A frugal man, Jarvis lived in a primitive cabin that he constructed from rock and the limbs trimmed from cut masts on his property.

Once, when Jarvis returned to the Vermont logging camp from a successful sales trip, he carried a pouch heavy with gold coins. From the contents of the pouch, he paid his workers. One of Jarvis's employees, a loyal worker named Hampton, commented that it was dangerous to carry around such a large amount of gold and that someone might kill him for it. Hampton suggested to his boss that he place the money in a bank.

At this, Jarvis laughed and said he did not trust banks. Taking Hampton into his confidence, Jarvis explained that he buried his gold in a secret location just a few steps from his cabin.

As time passed and the mast-cutting business continued to flourish, Jarivs grew quite wealthy by New England standards. In spite of his fortune, however, he preferred to live in his crude cabin, and when he traveled to the coast to conduct business, he slept on the docks and ate the food he carried in a pouch. Jarvis was never known to drink, stay in hotels, or otherwise spend money.

On numerous occasions, Jarvis was followed by robbers on his return trips to Vermont, but he always managed to elude his trackers.

During summer 1748, Hampton told Jarvis that two of the loggers had often wondered aloud where their employer hid his gold. The next few weeks, Jarvis often spotted those two men watching him closely when they weren't working in the woods. At those times, Jarvis was careful not to approach his secret hiding place.

Several weeks following Hampton's warning, David Jarvis was killed. While overseeing the cutting of masts in a certain section of the forest, a falling tree struck the businessman, and he died instantly when his skull was crushed. According to observers, there was no warning, and the men cutting the tree were never identified. It was believed, but never proven, that Jarvis was murdered by the two men who had expressed interest in his gold.

Hampton tried vainly to continue supplying masts to the shipbuilders, but being unskilled at business, he soon abandoned his attempts. For several weeks, Hampton searched the area around Jarvis's cabin for the cache of buried coins, but was never able to find it. It has been recorded that others, most likely men who cut masts for Jarvis, dug dozens of holes in the ground near the old cabin, but they, too, came away empty-handed.

During the first decade of the 1900s, a Middlesex resident reported finding several gold coins near an old abandoned logging camp not far from the Winooski River. The coins had 1740s mint dates.

It is likely that the individual accidently stumbled onto a portion of Jarvis's cache, a fortune that could possible be worth a million dollars today.

The Old Spaniard's Mine

Vermont has never been known as a silver-producing state, but for the past two hundred years, stories and legends have circulated regarding the likely existence of a lost silver mine that supposedly contains a trove of ingots as well as a rich vein of the precious ore located somewhere near Wallingford.

During the summer of 1797, young Richard Lawrence was hunting squirrels not far from his home in the southeastern Vermont town of Chester. As Lawrence made his way through the dark woods, he accidentally stumbled into a crude camp. Two horses were contentedly grazing in a nearby glade, and a small fire burned in an adjacent clearing. Next to the fire lay an old man, apparently sleeping, and a number of saddlebags were piled beside him.

When Lawrence approached the figure, the old man rose up and reached for a stout club lying nearby. On seeing only the youngster, the old man dropped the club and lay back down, groaning in agony. Curious, young Lawrence came closer, taking tentative steps toward the stranger.

As he neared the man, Lawrence saw the old man's left forearm was broken and that he appeared to be in great pain. The old man told the boy he had fractured the arm the previous day from a fall off his horse. When Lawrence announced he would try and obtain some help from town, the old man begged the lad not to tell anyone of his presence in the woods.

Instead, Lawrence raced to his home and, finding no one about, secured some rags and a short, thin plank. Returning to the clearing in the woods, he tied the makeshift splint to the old man's broken forearm. This done, the stranger thanked the boy and, moments later, fell into a deep sleep.

While the stranger lay quietly sleeping, Lawrence poked some life into the small fire and cast about in search of some food. On opening one of the saddlebags, he was startled to discover it was filled with shining bars of heavy metal. One after another the bags were opened, and all contained similar gleaming lengths of metal carefully packed into the wide panniers. Finding only a few provisions, Lawrence soon had a boiling pot of tea ready.

Sometime later when the old man awakened and drank some tea, he expressed his gratitude to the boy. Glancing toward the open saddlebags, he asked Lawrence if he knew what they contained. The boy admitted to looking into the bags and finding what he thought was silver. At that point, the old man told him an amazing story. As he held his sore forearm close to his chest, the old man told Lawrence he was a Spaniard, and the silver in his saddlebags had been dug from a mine about a two day's ride to the northwest. The silver, which he said was among the purest he had ever seen, was smelted in an oven just outside the mouth of the mine and poured into molds to form ingots. The silver bars in the saddlebags, the old man claimed, were only a small portion of the bullion, an accumulation from many years of hard work by several men, that remained in the cave.

When he was only a boy, said the Spaniard, he, along with several companions, worked as a crewman on a Spanish trading vessel that sailed up and down the Atlantic Coast. Running low on water and food, the captain of the ship ordered the anchor dropped in a quiet Massachusetts bay and sent a number of crewmen ashore to locate a fresh water spring and procure some game. The old man told Lawrence he was one of those crewmen. The captain told them that if they did not return in three days, the sails would be hoisted and the ship would continue up the coast toward a more likely site. While searching for water and game, the crewmen became lost and never found their way back to the ship. For months they wandered, eventually arriving in southern Vermont. While looking for shelter in a low mountain range, one of the men accidentally discovered an outcrop of silver.

After considerable discussion, the lost seamen agreed to remain and mine the silver. When they were satisfied with their accumulation, they promised they would attempt to make their way back to the coast and await rescue. Their intention was to return to Spain, procure a vessel of their own, and return for the silver.

Years passed, and the mine eventually extended into the side of the rocky hill for more than two hundred feet. The silver dug from the rock was smelted into ingots, which were then stacked like firewood against the walls of the mine. At last, when it was decided that each of the men possessed a fortune to take back to Spain, they covered the mine and struck out for the coast.

Along the way, two of the men died. After reaching the coast, they lived in crude shelters for nearly four months before catching the attention of a passing ship. During the trip back to Spain, two more of them succumbed to illness.

Once back in Spain, the survivors went about the business of trying to secure a ship to return to America and retrieve their wealth of silver. Weeks turned into months, and months into years. Finally, when enough money had been raised to commission a ship, the old man was the only surviving member of the original party of miners.

The Spaniard told Lawrence that the silver in the saddlebags represented all he was able to carry on the two horses he purchased in Boston on his recent arrival. It was likely, the old man told the boy, that he would never return to the mine.

The Spaniard placed a hand on young Lawrence's shoulder and expressed gratitude for his help. Then, to the boy's astonishment, the Spaniard gave him directions to reach the secret treasure mine, asking Lawrence not to try and retrieve any of the silver until he was old enough to appreciate its worth. The boy agreed. The next morning when Richard Lawrence walked out into the woods to the old man's campsite, the Spaniard was gone.

Years passed, and when Richard Lawrence was about twenty-five years old, he decided it was time to try to find the secret silver mine.

Recalling the directions entirely from memory, Lawrence rode horseback northwestward from Chester until reaching the hills described by the Spaniard so long ago. The hills in question turned out to be a portion of the southern extension of Vermont's Green Mountains. For several weeks, Lawrence lived in the hills near the present-day town of Wallingford while he searched for the mine, but he was never able to locate it. Finally, he returned to Chester where he told his story. Within a short time, dozens of men who had learned the tale of the old Spaniard's lost silver mine were searching the hills for riches.

Even with the increased number of people combing the area for the mine, its location continued to prove elusive. One of the searchers, a man experienced in geology, eventually determined the reason. Based on Lawrence's directions, the location of the silver mine was apparently buried under a heavy rockslide that had taken place sometime during the last ten years.

An organized attempt was made to remove some of the landslide debris, but the task proved much too formidable and the project was eventually abandoned.

To this day, no further efforts have been made to reach the Spanish silver mine. If the Spaniard's tale was true, and there is no reason to suspect otherwise, an incredible fortune in silver ingots still lies under tons of rock in the Green Mountains.

A Rebel Soldier's Treasure Tale

Few Americans are aware that a Vermont town was raided by a small company of Confederates in 1864. It is less well known that these soldiers, hundreds of miles from Dixie, also robbed three banks of just over $200,000 in gold coins, most of which was buried and never retrieved. The following tale was gleaned from the diary of a Rebel soldier who took part in the raid.

Just before dawn on the morning of October 18, 1864, twenty-five Confederate soldiers led by Captain Bennet H. Young rode out of Quebec toward the sleeping village of St. Albans in north-western Vermont. The Rebels, intent on sacking the three local banks, planned to escape back into Canada, and eventually transport the booty to the Confederate treasury that, at the time, was located in Virginia. Three days earlier, Confederate intelligence revealed that several recent large deposits in gold coins had been made, and, with the Rebel government badly in need of funds to purchase arms and ammunition, Young's command was ordered to loot the banks.

Just as the morning sun broke over the tree-lined horizon, the raiders galloped into town, forced their way into the banks, and stuffed $200,000 in gold coins into a number of saddlebags. This done, they strapped the heavy bags onto several horses they took from a nearby pen. After looting the banks, the Rebels, now yelling and shooting off their weapons, set fire to them.

The early morning commotion awoke several citizens of St. Albans who poured into the streets shouting warnings and firing at the raiders. None of the Confederate soldiers were struck, but two of the residents were shot down, one fatally. Within thirty minutes, the soldiers, $200,000 richer, whipped their mounts back up the road, hoping to reach the Canadian border before an effective pursuit could be organized.

Within an hour after the robbery, however, approximately twenty-five angry St. Albans citizens were armed, mounted, and riding after the raiders.

During the flight to Canada, the Confederates experienced problems maintaining a close herding of the pack animals that were carrying the loot. On several occasions, some horses broke away and had to be chased down and returned to the main herd. At least twice, the command was stopped when two of the hastily secured saddlebags with the gold coins broke loose and fell to the ground.

Aware that these recurring problems slowed down the escape, Captain Young ordered seven sacks removed from the mounts and buried in a nearby pine grove about two miles south of the Canadian border. This done, the command continued northward, the pursuit close on its heels.

Young's destination was Montreal, but after traveling only three miles into Canada, the Confederates were overtaken by the St. Albanites who disregarded the international border. After three soldiers fell to Yankee bullets, Young ordered his troops to turn and fight the hostile mob. During the subsequent skirmish, ten Confederates were killed, eleven captured, and three escaped. Only $80,000 worth of gold coins was found among the captured soldiers.

Though the St. Albanites searched the road for the rest of the day between the town and the point where the Confederates were overtaken, no sign of the stolen money could be found. The search continued for weeks, but was finally abandoned when it appeared hopeless.

Though chronicled, the St. Albans raid was regarded as a minor event in Vermont history, and, save for those who lost money and property, it was soon forgotten.

Then in 1868, a diary taken from the body of an ex-Confederate soldier, who had recently died in Mississippi from tuberculosis, provided a remarkable detail of the St. Albans raid and the subsequent caching of a portion of the loot. This discovery renewed interest in the stolen gold.

According to the diary, the dead soldier was one of the three Rebels who escaped the St. Albans posse. Keeping to the woods and evading settlements, he eventually made his way southwestward until he reached the Ohio River. Here, he obtained a series of boat rides to the Mississippi River. After constructing a crude raft, he floated southward with the current until finally reaching his home in Greenville, Mississippi.

The dead soldier's diary described the hiding place of the seven saddlebags. The cache, a deep hole located in the middle of a pine grove a short distance west of the St. Albans-Montreal road, was covered with a large flat rock that took three men to move.

The diary passed through the hands of several owners until eventually falling into the possession of one Hubert Crane in 1908. Crane, an Alabama resident, was deeply interested in Civil War history and was obsessed with the possibility of locating the buried gold cache. As soon as he was able to make the appropriate arrangements, Crane traveled to Vermont.

After checking into a hotel in St. Albans, Crane walked the streets of the town, asking the residents questions about the 1864 raid.

One evening as Crane dined at a local restaurant, he was approached by an old man who requested permission to sit with him and said he had a story to tell about the buried gold.

As Crane listened, the old man related that sometime in the year 1868, a stranger arrived at St. Albans and checked into the same hotel where Crane himself was registered. Like Crane, the newcomer asked many questions about the stolen gold and the events of the 1864 robbery, but otherwise remained reserved.

The stranger, who had a Southern accent, rented a horse and wagon and spent most of each day north of town in the woods alongside the road that led to Quebec. Occasionally, he was seen digging in a grove of pines located about two miles south of the Canadian border.

One day, a suspicious farmer approached the stranger and demanded to know what he was doing. The stranger provided only evasive answers and appeared to be confused and unsure of himself. Days passed, and the Southerner eventually departed.

According to Crane, the old man who told him the story believed the stranger was one of the three escaped Confederate soldiers and had returned to retrieve the cache of gold coins. Unfortunately, he was never able to relocate it. The old man admitted to searching throughout the pine grove for the treasure but was never successful.

When Crane asked the old-timer if he could take him to the place where the stranger had searched for the cache forty years earlier, he consented. An hour later, Crane and the old man were riding north out of St. Albans in a rented horse-drawn carriage.

Arriving at the approximate site of the cache, both men were stunned to discover that a recent forest fire had destroyed about two hundred acres of woods on the west side of the road. The pine grove no longer existed.

Together, Crane and the old man walked among the ashes and other debris from the fire in search of the large flat stone that allegedly covered the cache, but nothing could be found. Dejected, Crane returned to St. Albans, and on the following day he departed for his home in Alabama.

As far as anyone knows, the $120,000 in gold coins buried by the raiding Confederates has never been found, and to this day many believe it still lies beneath a large flat rock just west of Interstate 89 in Franklin County near the Canadian border.

The *Nebuchadnezzar's* Sea Chests

According to legend, four wooden chests filled with gold coins are buried near Bristol, Vermont. The treasure cache, if found, would likely be worth millions today, and many who have researched this tale are convinced it is true.

Phillip DeGrau was one of a number of sailors who worked aboard the *Nebuchadnezzar*, a trading vessel that did a brisk business from Nova Scotia to South Carolina along the Atlantic Coast. Charles Benoit, the *Nebuchadnezzar's* captain, was a ruthless commander, and rare was the day when two or three sailors were not tied to a mast and whipped for some minor infraction. Bloody Charles, as Benoit was called, had on occasion executed sailors he deemed troublesome, and DeGrau had felt the sting of Benoit's lash on more than one occasion.

Benoit, in spite of being a cold-blooded and pitiless ship captain, was a shrewd businessman, and it was reported he had grown wealthy as a result of his trading ventures. With each delivery, Benoit demanded payment in gold coins, and in time managed to fill several wooden chests that he stored in his cabin aboard ship.

From time to time, DeGrau and other sailors serving on the *Nebuchadnezzar* talked quietly about slaying Benoit and taking over the vessel. Ultimately, however, they feared Bloody Charles and his cruel officers sufficiently to postpone their plans.

During one trading voyage in 1765, the *Nebuchadnezzar* dropped anchor in Boston Harbor for a few days to take on provisions. While the seamen were ordered to remain on board under the watch of three armed officers, Benoit and a select group of friends went ashore to enjoy the pleasures of Boston's dockside taverns.

On the second afternoon at anchor, DeGrau and his companions decided that, with Benoit absent, the time was right to take over command of the ship. Following several clandestine meetings, the ten sailors remaining aboard the vessel quickly developed plans.

That night, as one of Benoit's officers stood guard on deck, he was suddenly attacked and killed by five of the sailors. The two other officers, who had retired to their bunks below, were beheaded as they slept. The three men's bodies were thrown overboard.

As DeGrau prepared to raise the anchor and hoist the sails for departure, several of the mutinous sailors expressed concern they would be pursued and quickly overtaken, captured, and executed on the spot. Benoit, they reminded DeGrau, was extremely well connected to a number of military and business leaders in Boston and would be able to initiate pursuit immediately.

As the sailors fretted more and more over their chances for escape, an idea occurred to DeGrau. He suggested they take the chests filled with gold coins and flee toward the interior of the continent. There, far from the influence of Benoit, they might travel into Canada and find a suitable place to settle with their newly obtained riches. All agreed this was a worthy plan, and two longboats were lowered into the waters of the harbor as DeGrau, accompanied by five others, broke into Benoit's cabin and dragged eight heavy wooden treasure-filled chests to the edge of the deck.

Because of the great weight of the chests, only four of them, along with the sailors, could be transported in the two longboats. In the dark of night, the men rowed to an isolated beach south of Boston, unloaded their fortune from the boats, and dragged the heavy chests to a location just above the line of high tide. While six sailors stood guard over the gold, DeGrau and three others crept into town, stole two stout wagons along with teams of horses to pull them, and returned to the beach just before dawn. After loading two chests onto each of the wagons, the sailors turned westward, driving the horses along a trail that wound away from the shore and into the forest.

For days the seamen traveled, constantly scanning the trail behind them for signs of pursuit. After three weeks, they decided they had made a clean escape, and their conversations turned to the life of luxury they would likely live when they reached their Canadian destination.

While crossing the Green Mountains of Vermont, one wagon broke down, and the heavy cargo was placed into the other. With only a single wagon now transporting the great weight of the four wooden gold-filled chests, travel slowed to a crawl. It took almost two weeks to cross the low mountain range.

By the time the seamen arrived on the west-facing slope of the Green Mountains, they determined that to continue under the present circumstances would be impossible. They decided to hide the chests, locate another wagon to facilitate transportation of the treasure, and resume their journey. After burying the four gold-filled chests in the floor of a shallow cave in the exposed rock face of a low mountain, the sailors closed the opening with rocks and forest debris. This done, they continued along the trail in search of a settlement.

The following day, they arrived at a tiny community of farmers and herders called Pocock. To their disappointment, the seamen discovered there were no wagons available in the entire town. After resting for a time, they decided to continue on foot to Canada, select a place to settle, and then return for the gold. A few days later, carrying several day's worth of food and supplies provided by the friendly townspeople, the men proceeded north-ward.

Whatever became of the sailors and their plans will likely never be known, for they never returned, as a group, to retrieve the four treasure-filled chests hidden in a small Green Mountains' cave.

In 1790, a somewhat stooped, elderly man arrived in Pocock riding a swaybacked, bony horse. Speaking in French, he managed to rent a small room from one of the townspeople and explained he wished to explore around the foothills of the Green Mountains. He told them his name was DeGrau.

For the next three months, DeGrau searched the canyons and ridges of the western slope of the nearby Green Mountains, trying to relocate the cave where the chests were hidden. As time passed, the residents of Pocock grew more and more curious about the strange visitor and began following him into the mountains. Time and again, DeGrau chased them away, cursing them for their intrusion. Finally, several townspeople confronted DeGrau and threatened to beat him unless he explained his actions. Faced with this threat, as well as suffering from discouragement at not being able to find the gold, the former sailor related the story of stealing the treasure chests and hiding them in a cave in the mountains.

For several weeks afterward, Pocock residents by the dozen combed the foothills in search of a cave, but they could not find one. Eventually, DeGrau returned to Canada, never to be seen again, and the Pocock searchers finally gave up looking for the treasure.

For decades it remained a mystery why so many searchers could not find DeGrau's treasure cave. Then, in 1870, a Middlebury resident, long fascinated with this tale of DeGrau's buried treasure, discovered a reference to an earthquake that struck the region on November 18, 1766. The quake, it was reported, caused a number of rockslides along the western slope of the Green

Mountains. The rockslides, according to researchers, likely covered DeGrau's treasure cave under tons of rubble.

Today, Pocock is known as the historic town of Bristol. The area where so many searched, and continue to search, for De-Grau's four gold-filled treasure chests, is referred to as the Bristol Money Diggings.

The Lost Steamboat

Not all treasures come in the form of gold and silver coins, ingots, or jewelry. Certain historical artifacts from a time when the United States was a much younger nation can command extremely high prices on the open market, and these days many professional treasure hunters spend their time hunting such things instead of lost mines and buried caches. Somewhere at the bottom of Lake Morey in Orange County may lie such a treasure in the form of what many scholars believe to be the country's first steamboat.

To some, it is common knowledge that Robert Fulton created the world's first steamboat. Careful research into the history of steamboats would reveal, however, that while Fulton was indeed the first person to make steamboat transportation a commercial endeavor, he himself credited other steamboat pioneers—John Fitch, James Rumsey, and William Symington among them—with the actual invention.

In 1807, Fulton supervised the completion of the *Clermont*, a large steamboat designed to haul freight and passengers up and down the Hudson River from New York to Albany and back. The undertaking was a success, and Fulton had other significant accomplishments in businesses associated with steamboating, freighting, and ferrying. His fame, however, was always attached to his initial steamboat venture.

Nineteen years before the *Clermont*'s completion, Samuel Morey, a Vermont resident, constructed what many researchers now believe to be the very first steamboat in the United States. Morey, financing his own project, designed and constructed a vessel that he piloted up and down a body of water that has come to be called Lake Morey near the small town of Fairlee. The lake is a half-mile from the Connecticut River, which separates Vermont from New Hampshire.

Morey's vessel differed from Fulton's in a number of ways. It was considerably smaller and could barely accommodate two people. Morey, who worked for a number of years on his invention, told observers it was merely a prototype, and that other, larger boats were planned. Morey explained to many that he intended to make steamboating a commercial success.

For years, Morey tried to get investors interested in his steamboat, explaining the potential of steam-driven transportation along the nation's rivers and coasts, even across the ocean to Europe. Hardly anyone had ever heard of Morey, a relatively unimposing man who was unskilled at business, and he met with failure after failure. Ever hopeful of success, and ultimately wealth, Morey persisted.

Unlike Morey, Robert Fulton was well-connected with politicians, military leaders, and a number of New York financiers. Because of his numerous successful inventions and enterprises, Fulton was on speaking and business terms with Napoleon, Robert Livingston, the American Minister to France, and wealthy financier Nicholas J. Roosevelt. Fulton's successful business enterprises, combined with his high position in the political and financial community and contacts in American and European social circles, made him the obvious choice for a steamboating venture.

When the Clermont was finally launched, newspapers throughout the country headlined the news. For weeks, reports about the Clermont and the new and growing steamboat business in America were topics of interest. In every case, Fulton was credited with being the brains behind the steamship industry.

When Samuel Morey learned of Fulton's steamboat successes and the attention lavished on him, he was initially envious and then grew bitter and dejected. He saw Fulton's star rise and new entrepreneurial offers arrive almost daily. Morey spent his days wondering what his life would have been like if his invention instead of Fulton's had been noticed by the businessmen and financiers.

A few months after the Clermont slid from New York City's shipbuilding docks into the Hudson River, Samuel Morey climbed into his own steamboat, fired the engine, and guided the vessel toward the middle of the large Vermont lake.

Morey scuttled his boat on the lake, and as it sank to the bottom, the inventor, clinging to a plank, paddled back to shore. Later, standing on a low hill overlooking the lake, Morey glanced one last time at the place where his steamship went down, turned, and walked away. Morey was seldom heard from again.

Today, expensive homes and at least two golf courses line the shores of Lake Morey, and a resort atmosphere pervades the area.

In 1990, two salvage operators encountered a reference to Samuel Morey's steamboat and its subsequent sinking. After examining the lake, the two men determined that the likelihood of the vessel remaining relatively intact beneath the waters was good. They began to make plans to locate the boat, raise it, and auction it off to dealers and collectors of Americana.

While preparations for the salvage operation were going on, one of the salvors was killed in a boating accident near the New York coast, and the plans were shelved by his partner for eighteen months. When the remaining salvor finally announced his plans to raise Morey's steamboat and sell it, state officials informed him that, as an historical artifact, the vessel would immediately become the state's property. When the salvor offered to raise it for the state for a fee, he was turned down.

Samuel Morey's boat, likely the first steamboat ever built in the United States, still lies at the bottom of Lake Morey.

NEW HAMPSHIRE

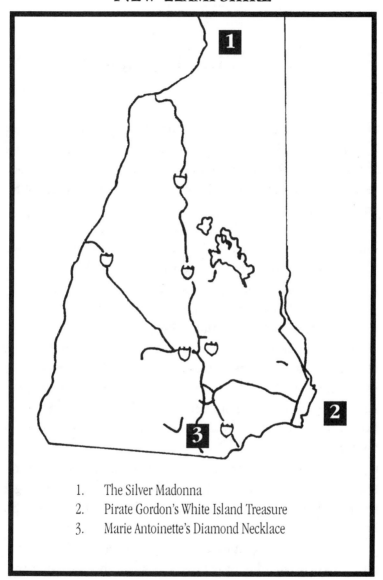

1. The Silver Madonna
2. Pirate Gordon's White Island Treasure
3. Marie Antoinette's Diamond Necklace

The Silver Madonna

One of the most coveted and sought after lost treasures of New England is the Silver Madonna, a two-and-a-half foot tall statue of the Virgin reputedly cast from pure silver and which once resided in a Catholic chapel in the Abanaki Indian village of St. Francis in Quebec.

Experts are hesitant to place a value on this amazing statue, all claiming the artifact, historically as well as monetarily, is priceless. Most agree, however, that the individual who finds this precious statue could easily command $1 million or probably more.

The Silver Madonna was stolen from the chapel by Major Robert Rogers's soldiers during a heartless raid on the village, resulting from the growing violence of the French and Indian War. During the war, relations between the French Canadians and the British colonists became more tense along the Canadian border. As the tension grew, Lord Jeffery Armherst, Commander of British troops at Fort Ticonderoga near the New York-Vermont border, grew concerned about the increasing number of raids regularly inflicted by the French and their Indian allies. In response, Armherst ordered Major Roberts and his crack ranger troops to launch a counter raid against the Indian village of St. Francis.

As much as Armherst detested Major Rogers and his undisciplined and insubordinate fighters, he was only too aware that these battle-scarred and experienced rangers were likely the only soldiers who could possibly carry out this assignment. Rogers's

Rangers, as they became known, disdained uniforms and taking orders, and some people regarded them as little more than hired killers.

About four hours before dawn some twenty-two days after being sent out by Armherst, Rogers and his nearly two hundred men silently surrounded the tiny village of St. Francis. Just as the faint light of dawn began to spread across the village clearing, Rogers fired his musket, signaling the attack. All at once, the rangers streamed into the village and pulled the Indians from their shelters. Practically defenseless, the Abenakis were clubbed, shot, and stabbed. No mercy was given to the members of the tribe. Men, women, and children were slaughtered, and even the priest was killed.

After only fifteen minutes, approximately two hundred Indians lay dead about the village. As several rangers scalped and mutilated the corpses, another two dozen stormed the chapel and sacked it, taking golden chalices and candlesticks, silver and gold crosses, and other items. Reaching the altar, the rangers suddenly stopped and stared in awe at the stunning figure of the Silver Madonna reflecting the flickering light of the flames now consuming a portion of the worship area. After a brief moment of hesitation, several of the men lifted the statue from its pedestal, carried it outside, and secured it firmly to the back of a pack horse.

Having carried out his assignment, Rogers quickly assembled his troops. Fearing pursuit and retaliation from the French when they learned of the raid, he led the rangers out of the village and to the trail that led back to Fort Ticonderoga. Approximately thirty men rode horses, but the majority were afoot. Supplies and munitions were strapped to pack horses. The last two horses in the retreating file transported the Silver Madonna and the treasures from the chapel.

After two hours on the trail, a rear scout alerted Rogers that a force of French soldiers, accompanied by one hundred Indians, was approaching at a rapid rate. Knowing his men were weary from the long march to St. Francis and from the battle, Roberts decided to split up the company and flee in different directions to confuse the pursuers. Rogers led just over half of his troops southward while the remaining rangers left the trail and proceeded due east through the forest. The latter group led the pack horses transporting the Silver Madonna and the church treasures.

The pursuing French and Indians were not confused at all by Rogers's tactic. With no hesitation, they likewise divided and continued in pursuit of each group of rangers with renewed vigor. Within minutes, the French and Indians overtook both groups of rangers. Initially, stragglers were easily shot and killed, but as the French closed in, hand-to-hand fighting was common with the attackers taking a heavy toll.

The party of rangers traveling eastward fared the worst. After two days of fleeing and fighting, the French and their Indian companions killed about forty rangers. With the enemy close at their heels, the escaping troops had no time to rest or eat. To complicate matters, an early snowstorm struck the area and caught the unprepared rangers by surprise. Soldiers began deserting at every opportunity, often walking away from fleeing rangers and entering the dense woods.

Arriving at the lower end of Lake Memphremagog on the Quebec-Vermont border, the horse carrying the chalices and candlesticks pulled up lame. Rather than take precious time to transfer the cargo or bury the treasures, the rangers simply abandoned the animal and its load, crossed the lake, and proceeded southeastward toward the Connecticut River.

The party of rangers continued to dwindle from starvation, desertion, and death at the hands of the pursuers, and it was a much smaller and more ragged, tired, and hungry group that plodded through the Vermont woods just ahead of the French soldiers. By the time they reached the banks of the Connecticut River, the rangers numbered only four. They carried no food—only their guns—but they continued to lead the weary horse which was transporting the Silver Madonna.

One of the rangers, Sergeant Amos Parsons, had visited this region years earlier and claimed he could lead his companions to safety. After crossing the Connecticut River in New Hampshire near the present-day town of Lancaster, the tired soldiers followed the Israel River upstream into the foothills of the White Mountains. After three more days of slow and very difficult hiking, the men were reduced to eating the leather of their buckskins for sustenance. Finally, halted by exhaustion and starvation, they climbed a steep, switchbacking path from the riverbank to the shelter of an overhanging rock. Here, they killed the horse carrying the Madonna, eagerly drank its warm blood, and consumed the flesh raw.

Just before dawn the following morning, two of the men awoke with severe stomach cramps, and Parsons raged with delirium brought on by the ordeal. Spotting the Silver Madonna, which had been set upright near one corner of the shelter, Parsons decided the statue carried a curse with it and that the object was responsible for the recent trials from which so many of his companions suffered and died. Maniacally, Parsons seized the statue, dragged it to the edge of the bank, and rolled it into the Israel River. After watching the heavy silver statue sink beneath the water of the stream, the deranged Parsons, now screaming and pulling at his matted hair, ran down the steep path and into the woods, never to be seen again.

For two days, the three remaining soldiers lingered under the rock shelter. On the third morning, one of the men awoke to find his companions dead. Confused and weak, he left the shelter and followed the faint path in an upstream direction. About two hours after dawn the next day, he wandered into a tiny settlement, and its residents fed him. Several weeks passed before the ranger regained his health, but his mind had apparently snapped from his terrible experience and he eventually went insane.

As the ranger was being ministered to, he told the citizens about the raid on the Abenaki village, stealing the Silver Madonna, the flight from the French soldiers through the Connecticut woods, and his companions' deaths. In great detail, he related how he laid in a far corner of the shelter and watched quietly as Sergeant Parsons rolled the Silver Madonna into the Israel River.

Several weeks later, four of the men from the settlement traveled along the banks of the Israel River until they located the rock shelter described by the ranger. Inside, they discovered the remains of two men and a horse.

The cherished Silver Madonna has never been recovered. It is believed by everyone who has researched this tale that it still lies at the bottom of the Israel River near a point close to the rock shelter. Given the statue's significant weight, it is unlikely that it traveled far downstream from the point that it entered the river. Considering the river bottom's texture in this area, it is highly likely that the object sank to a depth of several feet below the bed. The point along the Israel River where Sergeant Parsons is believed to have rolled the statue into the stream has been determined to be just downstream from the town of Jefferson.

Lying only a few feet beneath the surface of the Israel River remains one of the most cherished artifacts of the French and Indian War, and one that is worth well over a million dollars to collectors today.

Pirate Gordon's White Island Treasure

Some historians have referred to Sandy Gordon, an early eighteenth century pirate, as ruthless, evil, and fearless. Others have called him insane and offer as proof the fact that he blew himself up with his ship within a year after burying an incredible fortune in gold and silver coins that remains lost to this day on New Hampshire's White Island.

As a youth, Sandy Gordon was in trouble so often that his frustrated parents threw him out of their Glasgow, Scotland, house, leaving him to wander the streets and alleys of town fending for himself. Constantly running afoul of the law for stealing from shops and dockside warehouses, young Gordon had spent countless weeks in the Glasgow jail by the time he was eighteen.

One afternoon during spring 1704, Gordon, while loitering around the docks waiting for an opportunity to steal something, was offered a job as a crewman aboard a merchantman, the *Porpoise*. Thrilled with the possibilities of sailing the high seas and visiting new countries, Gordon signed on.

After only a few days at sea, Gordon grew increasingly disappointed as he discovered his job involved little more than scrubbing decks, painting wooden fixtures, and polishing brass fittings. Growing increasingly bored, Gordon began casting about for some diversion and was soon entertaining himself by stealing from his fellow crewmen.

John Herring, the *Porpoise*'s captain, brought his eighteen-year-old daughter, Martha, along on this particular voyage. In those days, a woman aboard a sailing ship was considered by many to be bad luck, and in this case it turned out to be so for Gordon. While daily performing his scrubbing, painting, and polishing duties, Gordon often positioned himself so he could carry on conversations with Martha Herring as she took her daily walks. In time, the two grew to be very friendly and eventually agreed to meet secretly one night. One evening after dinner, Gordon waited until well past midnight when he was certain everyone aboard ship was asleep, crept to Martha's cabin, and knocked quietly on her door. Martha opened it.

Captain Herring had long suspected Gordon had designs on his daughter. Herring, who never quite trusted Gordon, was also convinced he had been stealing from the other crewmen and sailors. Acting on a hunch, Herring burst into his daughter's cabin and caught the pair locked in an embrace.

The next morning, Gordon was tied to the mainmast, and Herring himself administered one hundred lashes. Before the captain was finished, Gordon had fallen unconscious, held upright only by his tight bonds. His naked back, ragged with flayed, hanging flesh, dripped tiny pools of blood, which gathered on the deck below his feet. After being cut down and having his wounds bound, Gordon was locked into manacles and placed in the ship's brig for thirty days.

On being released, Gordon returned to work on the decks, but he was told that he would be removed from the ship the first time it docked on the Atlantic Coast.

Gordon, seething with hatred for Captain Herring, plotted revenge as he scrubbed and painted. As the long days at sea passed, Gordon encountered kindred spirits, other laborers among the crew who, like himself, had felt the bite of Herring's whip and who also despised the captain. Together, they plotted a takeover of the *Porpoise*.

Three days later, the mutineers took control of the ship, and Herring, one of the first to be taken prisoner, was tied to the same mast where Gordon had received his whipping. Laughing and taunting all the while he wielded the whip, Gordon administered exactly one hundred lashes to the back of a stripped and naked Herring. The whipping nearly killed the captain. After the beaten man was cut down and lay bleeding on the deck, Gordon burned both his eyes out with a hot poker. According to some researchers, Gordon, now raving, hurled Herring overboard.

Now in control of the *Porpoise*, Gordon decided to become a pirate. With his fellow mutineers serving as a crew, he returned to the British Isles and European coast, plundering and pillaging ships and coastal communities during the next three years.

Several chests packed with gold and silver coins and jewelry were accumulated from the raids and stored in Gordon's cabin. He enjoyed this wealth and often gazed upon it, counting the coins for hours at a time. Many agree that it was during this time that Gordon began to grow markedly insane.

Although Gordon and his pirates had stolen millions of dollars' worth of treasure, the sailors and crewmen were paid very little, and most of them came to resent their captain. Eventually, Gordon's own crew mutinied, seized the chests of treasures, and cast him adrift in a rowboat off Scotland's south coast.

Finally reaching shore, Gordon found an old abandoned farmhouse and took refuge. A nearby spring afforded fresh water, and he lived on shellfish, which he plucked from the shallow ocean waters and shorebirds that he was able to club.

One afternoon in 1712, Gordon, hair and beard grown long and matted, was walking along the shore not far from the old farmhouse when he spotted a sailing vessel on the horizon. As he watched, the ship entered the tiny bay, dropped sail, and lowered anchor. Moments later, several men rowed a longboat toward the shore where he stood.

Beaching the craft, several crewmen, carrying water barrels, climbed out of the boat, approached Gordon, and asked where they could find some fresh water. Gordon led them to the spring.

As Gordon spoke with the newcomers, he learned they were pirates, and that their captain was none other than Edwin Teach, the notorious Blackbeard.

Though the pirates regarded Gordon as a bit mad and wished he would go away, they consented to his request to return to the ship with them. Once on board the vessel, Gordon asked for an audience with Blackbeard. When he was finally admitted to Teach's cabin, the filthy Gordon described his years of successful piracy and asked to join the noted brigand and return to sea. Blackbeard agreed to give Gordon a chance but told him that if he failed, he would be killed.

Gordon proved to be a skilled seaman and a fearless fighter. His skill in battle did not go unnoticed by Blackbeard, and the pirate leader attributed several raiding successes to the man he considered slightly mad. Eventually, Blackbeard rewarded him by giving him his own ship, a recently captured Spanish merchantman that Gordon renamed The Flying Scot.

Again on his own, Gordon, having acquired a competent crew, went about raiding along the European coast once again. Finally, with the hold of The Flying Scot filled with treasure estimated to be worth millions, Gordon decided to sail to America, find a suitable location to settle, and conduct raids on the trading vessels he knew frequented that area.

Eventually, Gordon arrived at White Island, located just off the coast of New Hampshire. The pirate liked the looks of the island, its solitude, and the fact that it could be easily defended.

He immediately ordered the construction of a sturdy cabin. Once the dwelling was completed, Gordon, over a period of several weeks and under cover of darkness, away from his crew's prying eyes, carried his fortune in gold and silver coins and jewelry from the ship to the rocky island and buried it somewhere near his cabin.

Gordon enjoyed life on White Island, and whenever he grew restless for adventure, he gathered up his crew and sailed *The Flying Scot* along the Atlantic Coast and conducted raids on communities and ships.

After residing on White Island for nearly a year, Gordon received word that a fleet of British man-o'-war ships were searching this portion of the Atlantic Coast for pirates. The British had orders to kill or capture any brigands they encountered and to seize all ships and cargo.

Early one morning as Gordon walked around White Island, he spied a fleet of ships sailing from the east. After watching them for a while, he discerned that they were British warships and appeared to be headed directly toward the small harbor where the pirate ship was anchored. Intent on escape, Gordon quickly alerted his crew to prepare *The Flying Scot* for a quick departure. As sails were hoisted and anchor raised, the pirate leader soon realized the British ships were dangerously close and that there was no time for flight, only battle.

It was soon obvious to Gordon that he was heavily outnumbered. Determined not to be taken alive and hanged, Gordon seized a burning torch, climbed into the ship's magazine, and ignited the store of powder. Instantly, *The Flying Scot* exploded, a fiery, concussive blast that hurled burning timbers and men a hundred yards in all directions. All aboard the ship, including Gordon, were killed instantly, and all that remained of *The Flying*

Scot were pieces of decking and hull floating on the surface of the water near White Island.

No one was left alive who new the location of Gordon's secret treasure cache. Today, this buried fortune is estimated to be worth several million dollars.

Marie Antoinette's Diamond Necklace

Pennichuck Pond is a small glacial lake located about two-and-a-half miles from downtown Nashua, New Hampshire. The pond, a half-mile long and nearly a quarter-mile wide, is fed by the cold waters of Pennichuck Brook. According to legend, somewhere along the shore of Pennichuck Pond lies buried one of the most incredible treasures in the United States—a fabulous diamond necklace believed to have been commissioned by Marie Antoinette in France in 1788.

One of several small lakes in this area formed by the erosive and scouring action of Pleistocene glaciers that passed over the bare rock tens of thousands of years ago, Pennichuck Pond is located in the heart of timber country, and sometimes served as a source of fresh water for nearby logging camps.

Marie Antoinette, originally from Austria and sister to Emperor Leopold, was the wife of King Louis XVI, the French monarch who reigned from 1774 to 1792. French citizens considered Marie Antoinette quite frivolous and ill-suited for her high position in society.

In 1788, Marie Antoinette contracted with a highly skilled jeweler in France to design and create the most exquisite diamond necklace in the world. Emissaries were sent throughout Europe to search for and obtain the finest diamonds available, and the ultimate piece of finely crafted jewelry was described as a stunning necklace of extraordinary beauty containing dozens of large and magnificently cut gems. The cost to Marie Antoinette was in excess of the French equivalent of $1 million.

The French Revolution, which lasted from 1789 to 1799, eventually overthrew the absolute monarchy of King Louis XVI. As popular discontent rose during the early part of 1789, Marie Antoinette grew concerned that the French peasants would take her precious jewels and other belongings. As the pace of the Revolution picked up, Marie Antoinette carefully packed her necklace up in a small metal box that she then stuffed into the middle of a wooden trunk containing a number of other items. This trunk, along with several others, was shipped to Canada. At the time, hundreds of Frenchmen were living in eastern Canada, and the political sympathies of many were still with the ruling government.

In France, the Revolution erupted into a bloody war, and Antoinette was eventually executed by guillotine on October 16, 1793.

The necklace's recipient still remains a mystery. Around 1790, a Frenchman, accompanied by an Indian, transported a wooden trunk from Canada across the border into Maine, ultimately arriving by wagon in the New Hampshire settlement of Nashua near the Massachusetts border.

At Nashua, the Frenchman and Indian set up a temporary camp just outside of town for several days while they rested from their long journey. While in camp, they closely guarded the wooden trunk. When one of them went into town to purchase a few supplies, the other remained in camp, standing guard over the trunk and keeping passers-by and visitors from coming near it.

After one week, the two men packed their wagon and rode away from town toward the northwest along a well-traveled road. Though the strangers had barely spoken with anyone in town, the

Nashua residents presumed they were simply continuing on their journey and leaving the area for good.

After traveling only a little over two miles, however, the newcomers turned off the road toward the southwest and guided their wagon along a logging trail that paralleled Pennichuck Brook. Several minutes later, they encountered Pennichuck Pond, a clear lake surrounded by dense woods. Perceiving the location as suitable, the two men then busied themselves with building a small log cabin.

Once the cabin was constructed, the wooden trunk was placed in one corner and covered with a blanket and a few household items.

Living near the shore of Pennichuck Pond, the Frenchman and the Indian occasionally hunted game, and once every six weeks or so one of the men went to town to replenish supplies. They received few visitors at their residence and earned, rightfully so, a reputation for being recluses.

Two years following the arrival of the strangers, the Indian had to return to Canada on a family matter. Following his friend's departure, the Frenchman grew concerned about the security of the wooden trunk in the cabin. He worried that some uninvited visitor might steal it when he needed to go into town to purchase supplies. On the occasions when he did ride to Nashua, the Frenchman fretted for the entire trip about the safety of the wooden trunk and its contents. On the way back to the cabin, he whipped the team of horses to top speed and never relaxed until he ascertained the trunk was indeed safe inside the cabin. The Frenchman only stopped worrying when the Indian returned about four months later.

During the next few years, the Indian left for Canada on at least three other occasions. Each time his friend rode away, renewed concern about the trunk's safety gripped the Frenchman.

Shortly after the Indian departed on one of his Canadian visits, the Frenchman decided to find a suitable hiding place for the trunk in order to ease his conscience and concern about having to leave it at times. He dragged it down the slight incline toward the pond and buried it not far from the shoreline. To mark the cache, he rolled a large rock on top of it. After returning to the cabin, the Frenchman located his journal and made an entry describing the hiding place of the chest.

While the Indian was away, the Frenchman took ill. Weakened from pneumonia, he could scarcely rise from his pallet and found it impossible to go into town for help. For several days he fought the illness, but it was too much for him and he eventually succumbed.

When the Indian returned, his friend had been dead for several weeks. After burying the Frenchman, the Indian decided to go back to Canada for good and began packing some items into the wagon. As he did so, he noticed that the trunk was missing. For the next two days, the Indian hiked throughout the nearby woods and along the lake shore in search of it but could find nothing. Finally giving up, he climbed aboard the wagon and rode away toward Canada.

Twenty years later, the old Indian returned to Nashua. He walked from store to store and house to house asking people if they had known the Frenchman who once lived out near Pennichuck Pond. Since the Frenchman only rarely came into town, and seldom conversed with anyone when he did, few recalled him. Eventually, the constable arrested the Indian for being a nuisance and kept him in the town jail for a week. During the time the Indian was incarcerated, he related a most amazing story to the lawman.

After burying his friend, the Indian returned to Canada to live with relatives. Approximately ten years later, he discovered the

Frenchman's journal among his belongings in an old canvas bag. Perusing the journal, the Indian came across the reference to the buried trunk and the rock marker near the shoreline of Pennichuck Pond.

A variety of family-related problems interfered with his immediate return to Pennichuck Pond, but after the passage of another ten years, the Indian, now somewhat elderly, borrowed a horse and departed for Nashua to try and find the trunk.

His journey was a difficult one and lasted for several weeks. At times he became lost and often went without food for days. Finally, he arrived at Pennichuck Pond and moved into the remains of the old cabin he helped construct more than two-and-a-half decades earlier. The roof was partially fallen in and one wall leaned precariously outward, but the Indian found it suitable.

Walking from the cabin to the shore of the lake, the Indian was surprised to find dozens of large rocks scattered about, any one of which could have served as a marker for the buried trunk.

After digging under several rocks over the next few days, the Indian grew extremely tired and frustrated and decided to go into town. Once in town, he tried to find anyone who might have known the Frenchman and might be able to provide some information about the trunk, but alas, it was not to be.

The constable listened intently to the Indian's tale, and when the prisoner had finished, the lawman leaned in close to him and asked what was in the trunk.

The Indian told him the trunk contained a metal box that, in turn, held Marie Antoinette's long lost diamond necklace that the dead Frenchman had been given the responsibility of protecting.

The following morning, the constable released the Indian from the jail cell, and the two rode out to Pennichuck Pond. After showing the lawman the old log cabin, the Indian pointed to the rock shore of the lake. Somewhere under one of those stones, he said, was buried the priceless diamond treasure.

Day after day for nearly two weeks, the Indian and the constable dug into the soft sediments along the shore of Pennichuck Pond, but never found the chest. One day, the Indian simply disappeared without a word, and it was presumed he went back to Canada. He was never seen again in Nashua.

On his own, the constable returned to the lake shore from time to time searching for the chest, but after several months of effort with nothing to show for it, he finally gave up.

The story of the buried diamond necklace soon spread throughout much of New England, and occasionally someone would show up in Nashua asking directions to Pennichuck Pond. Though a succession of treasure hunters arrived in the region over the next several decades, no significant discovery was ever reported.

In 1983, a group of Boy Scouts camped along the shore of Pennichuck Pond for two days and nights. During the day, activities including hiking, woodsmanship, and boating occupied the youngsters and their leaders, and dinner and campfire stories filled the evenings.

While several scouts and scoutmasters prepared a large meal on the second evening of the outing, a trio of boys were spotted throwing rocks at a makeshift target they had erected not far from camp. When one of the leaders called the boys to dinner, he noticed their target was constructed of several slats of wood that appeared to be very old and rotted. One of the slats had a metal fitting—the kind often found attached to the corner of a wooden trunk—fixed to one end. After examining the pieces of wood and determining they were, indeed, parts from a trunk or sea chest, the scout leader asked the boys where they had obtained them. Pointing to an area near the waterline of the lake, the scouts explained they found them sticking out of the dirt.

The scoutmaster was familiar with the tale of the lost Marie Antoinette necklace and wondered if the pieces of trunk might be somehow connected.

Since it was dusk and dinner was ready, the scout leader decided to wait until morning to have the youths show him precisely where they found the pieces of wood.

Early the next day, however, the scouts could not identify the exact location where they found the wood. After about two hours of searching along the shoreline, the leader, with the help of several more scouts, failed to find anymore pieces of the trunk.

Could the wood the Boy Scouts found have been part of the trunk in which the long lost Marie Antoinette necklace had been buried? Since Pennichuck Pond has seen little use and virtually no habitation in the area at all, it seems probable. If true, then the smaller metal box, containing the priceless piece of jewelry, may very well lie only a few inches below the surface, freed from the rotted wood of the trunk that it was buried in nearly two hundred years earlier!

If discovered, the diamond necklace would likely be worth several million dollars today.

MASSACHUSETTS

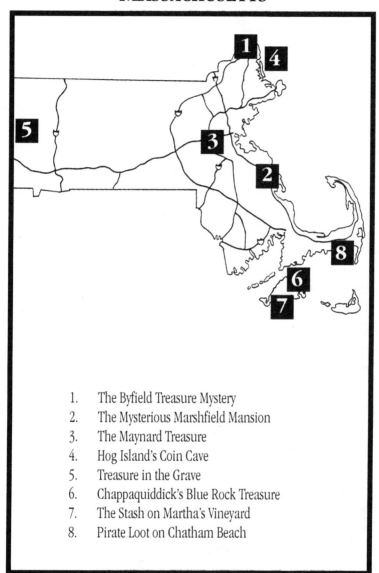

Pirate Loot on Chatham Beach

In the historic New England town of Chatham, Massachusetts, tourists mingle and flow through the picture-postcard streets. Located on the seaward side of the elbow-shaped peninsula, this small town near the Nantucket Sound harbors a mystery of buried, unearthed, and then lost again pirate treasure.

During the 1830s, John Eldridge, long-time resident of Chatham, owned the most successful tailor shop in the town. Well known in the town, Eldridge was respected by area residents as a hard worker who provided well for his small family.

Arthur Doane, a local fisherman and occasional laborer, was Eldridge's good friend and often stopped by the tailor shop to visit. One afternoon, Doane arrived while Eldridge was putting the finishing touches on a suit coat, and the two men chatted amiably for about an hour. On this particular visit, however, Doane appeared rather subdued and seemed preoccupied as Eldridge carried on the bulk of the conversation. Presently, Doane asked his friend if it were possible to exchange foreign coins for American money.

Eldridge replied that it was, and that there were banks, dealers, and collectors in Boston, Philadelphia, and elsewhere on the East Coast that could handle such transactions. Doane spoke very little during the next several minutes as Eldridge finished up the coat. As the tailor was putting away his material and thread, Doane made a curious request: He asked Eldridge if he would please exchange some foreign coins for him during his next visit to the city. The kindly tailor readily agreed, and Doane immediately pulled six gold pieces from his coat pocket. The coins, with 1810 mint dates, were of Spanish origin.

After examining the coins, Eldridge told his friend he would be glad to exchange them the next time he traveled to the city to purchase cloth. Naturally curious about the coins, Eldridge asked Doane where he got them, but the fisherman sheepishly replied that he preferred not to reveal the source at that time. He did insist, however, that they were obtained honestly. With that, Doane thanked his friend and departed.

About two weeks later, Eldridge traveled to Philadelphia on business. In the city, the tailor took Doane's coins to a collector, who said that they had a very high gold content. Eldridge was paid about five dollars for the lot.

When he returned to Chatham, Eldridge handed the money over to Doane who, in turn, paid a small amount to the tailor for his trouble. Once again, curiosity seized Eldridge, and he asked his friend about the source of the coins but was told not to be concerned. Doane reinforced his earlier statement—no dishonesty was involved.

Every few weeks thereafter, Doane brought six Spanish coins to Eldridge who took them to either Boston or Philadelphia where they would be exchanged for American money. This odd arrangement between the two friends continued regularly for forty-six years, and during that time, Eldridge estimated he returned approximately $60,000, an impressive fortune at the time, to Doane.

Shortly after Eldridge began exchanging money for his friend, Doane married, eventually had a son, and settled into a stable family life. The fisherman used his money to purchase newer and better equipment, improving his now thriving fishing enterprise. Doane also managed to save a considerable amount and was soon regarded as a wealthy man. Most Chatham residents simply assumed he made his fortune from fishing.

In 1880, Doane became very ill and was almost completely bedridden. By now, he was a widower, his only child had died, and Doane had lived alone for nearly two years. He seldom received visitors except for his physician, housekeeper, and John Eldridge. Realizing he did not have long to live, Doane summoned Eldridge to his sickroom. When the tailor arrived, Doane asked him to sit next to his bed so he could explain the story behind the gold coins.

About fifty years earlier, Doane was fishing off the coast of Chatham Beach when he decided to pull into port to visit a young girl he was enamored of. Because her father did not care for the young fisherman, Doane and the girl arranged to meet secretly on the beach. That night, while they were sitting among the dunes, they observed a rowboat land on the beach in the distance. Several men who were dressed like pirates climbed out of the rowboat, carrying a heavy chest and several shovels. They proceeded up the beach to a spot not far from where the two lovers were hidden behind a low bush.

After digging for about twenty minutes, the men lowered the chest into the hole, covered it up, returned to the boat, and rowed out to sea, presumably to an awaiting vessel that lay beyond sight in the darkness.

The following morning, Doane borrowed a spade and returned to a place near the site of the buried chest. For nearly an hour he hid behind a sand dune and scanned the horizon for some sign of the sailors who had visited the beach the previous night. Deciding that no one was watching, Doane began to dig, and after an hour of shoveling, his spade finally struck the top of the wooden chest. After several more minutes of effort, he forced open the container and, his heart pounding furiously with excitement and from exertion, Doane gazed down at nearly two dozen canvas bags tightly packed with gold Spanish coins.

Doane knew he needed to find a new hiding place for this fortune. Quickly, he closed the chest and refilled the hole before anyone could spot him at his activity. Scanning the horizon, he noticed a high, prominent sand dune about four hundred yards away. The dune began approximately thirty yards from the shoreline and extended about seventy yards toward the dirt road that led to Chatham. Doane decided he would rebury the treasure next to the large dune.

That evening just after sundown, Doane returned to the large dune and excavated a deep hole on the south side. Following this, he exhumed the treasure chest, removed all of the gold-filled sacks, and carried them to the new excavation. He returned for the chest and dragged it back to the large dune, lowered it into the new hole, and refilled it with the gold coins, keeping one sackful out for himself. Quickly, yet very carefully, he filled in the hole and smoothed over the sand.

For a few years, Doane nervously kept the secret of the buried treasure to himself, fearing that the men who originally buried it would return, find him out, and kill him. Having never had much money, Doane was uncomfortable about handling the incredible fortune he stumbled onto. Finally, after the passage of a few years, he felt reasonably certain he would not be detected, and he approached Eldridge about exchanging the coins for American money. The arrangement worked out fine for both men, and when he ran low on funds, Doane would simply return to the south side of the large dune at night and retrieve another sackful of gold.

As Doane lay dying in his bed, he pointed to a cherry wood dresser on the opposite side of the room and told Eldridge to look in the top drawer. On opening the drawer, the tailor found eighteen gold coins lying in the bottom, all that remained of

Doane's most recent acquisition. "When you need more," Doane told him, "you will have to go to the dune and dig them up." Growing weaker, Doane, in a halting, raspy voice, provided his friend with precise directions to the buried treasure chest.

The next morning, Eldridge made the short journey out to the beach and easily located the dune described by Doane. Carrying a spade and using the fisherman's directions, he paced off the necessary steps. When he arrived at the specified location, Eldridge proceeded to dig into the sand.

The tailor, not used to heavy work, paused often to catch his breath, and after about an hour of digging was finally relieved to hear the sound of his spade strike the top of the wooden chest.

After prying open the lid, Eldridge discovered seven sacks filled with gold coins. He removed one of them, closed the chest, and refilled the hole. The next day, he closed his tailor shop and traveled to Philadelphia where he sold the coins for a total of $4,500.

On returning to Chatham, Eldridge deposited the money in his bank account and rushed over to Doane's house to inform him. On arriving, however, he was told by the housekeeper that Arthur Doane had passed away the previous evening. Saddened by the loss of his friend, Eldridge remained depressed for several days as he worked quietly in his tailor shop.

One evening, about two weeks following Doane's death, Eldridge decided to walk out to the dune on the following morning and retrieve the remaining six sacks of coins. As he was preparing for bed, Eldridge closed his windows against an approaching storm. The horizon grew quite dark as a squall was rising, and the tailor silently prayed that all of the local fishermen had their boats moored tightly as a precaution against the rising winds and sea.

That night, one of the worst storms in Chatham's history blew in from the Atlantic Ocean and caused tremendous damage to boats, piers, and homes for many miles along the southern shore. The following morning as the sky cleared, Eldridge, carrying his spade, hiked to the beach. When he arrived at the approximate location of the sand dune, he was stunned to discover it had been completely washed away from the previous night's storm. His heart sank as he walked about the beach seeking any sign of the buried treasure, but he found none. At various spots, the tailor dug into the sand hoping to accidentally encounter the buried chest, but after a full day of searching, digging, and finding nothing, he returned home exhausted and discouraged.

On dozens of other occasions, Eldridge carried his shovel to the beach, searching for the buried chest. Time and again, he made excavations in places where he was certain he would locate the gold, but each time he encountered only failure.

The remaining sacks of gold coins were estimated to be worth approximately twenty-five thousand dollars in 1880 gold exchange rates. Today, such a treasure trove would be worth considerably more.

They are still there. Somewhere on the beach between the shoreline and the historic town of Chatham, the gold coins still lay inside the wooden chest just a few feet below the surface of sand.

The Byfield Treasure Mystery

For nearly a century and a half, two steamer trunks filled with gold British coins, each containing at least one hundred and thirteen grains of pure gold, lay buried near the town of Byfield in northeastern Massachusetts. Though a descendant of one of the men responsible for caching this incredible wealth possessed a map to the alleged site, she was unable to find the treasure. In 1932, however, evidence came to light that strongly suggested all or a portion of this buried fortune may have been recovered by a local resident—a poor laborer.

This tale has its beginnings in 1800. Captain Roger Hayman, a British sailor-turned-pirate, often visited the ports of the Caribbean and occasionally launched raiding expeditions from makeshift headquarters located on the west coast of Haiti. Hayman commanded a large fleet of pirate vessels—sometimes as many as fifteen—and attacked and pillaged virtually everything he encountered on the open sea and along the eastern seaboard of the United States. Hayman feared no one and never retreated from danger—he even attacked warships belonging to England and the United States.

During the last week of February in 1800, a war fleet consisting of four ships—three American and one British—arrived in the Caribbean searching for Hayman. The two governments, tired of losing ships and cargo to the notorious pirate, intended to put him out of business once and for all. England, like the United States, had been suffering depredations by Hayman for years and volunteered part of her navy to help bring him to justice.

Learning of the approaching fleet, the fearless Hayman ordered an armada of ten of his finest vessels and undertook an attack on the new arrivals. During the initial stages of the fighting, the pirates sank one of the American ships. As Hayman's vessel tied alongside the British ship, his pirates clambered aboard the ship. After killing most of the officers and crew, Hayman learned that the ship was transporting two large wooden chests filled with gold coins. The coins—minted between 1794 and 1799—were a portion of a large payroll intended for the British Navy.

Hayman quickly loaded the chests onto his own ship, and had no sooner secured them in the hold, when he was attacked by one of the remaining American vessels. During the subsequent battle, the pirate captain suffered nearly a dozen wounds.

Unable to command effectively, Hayman's forces fell into disarray, and the tide of the battle gradually shifted. Within a short time, the American ships sank three of the pirate vessels. Not liking this turn of events, Hayman ordered his crew to set sail for the open sea and in an attempt to outrun the Americans. As the pirate leader was planning his escape, the United States' fleet sank five more of the pirate ships and, save for Hayman's brig, captured the only one remaining afloat. This battle marked the end of the domination in the Atlantic and Caribbean waters by Roger Hayman and his band of cutthroats.

Once safely out in the Atlantic Ocean, Hayman and his crew sailed to England where they anchored off a remote part of the coast north of Liverpool. Hayman ordered the two treasure-filled trunks hauled to shore and buried and, following this, had the ship scuttled. The pirate then paid off all his men and sent them on their way. A few weeks later, Hayman had the chests unearthed and delivered to a new hideaway near downtown Liverpool.

At Liverpool, Hayman intended to rest with his wife and children and recover from his wounds before embarking on another piracy expedition on the high seas. On arriving, however, he discovered his family had migrated to New York, leaving a message for him to join them. Anxious to be with them, Hayman immediately arranged to sail to America in spite of his nagging wounds.

Three weeks later, Hayman supervised the loading of the two treasure chests onto the brig that would transport him to New York. As stewards negotiated the heavy trunks up the gangplank, the process was closely observed by two men lurking in the dockside shadows—a physician named Griffin and a businessman named Stearns Compton. Days earlier, the two men recognized Hayman and suspected the two large chests contained treasure. Silently, they watched as the trunks were dragged into the purser's cabin and the door locked tightly as Hayman stood by. The pirate, now in severe pain and growing weak from his wounds, was then escorted to his own cabin. Shortly thereafter, Griffin and Compton boarded the vessel.

Several days later as the ship sailed across the Atlantic Ocean toward America, Dr. Griffin was summoned by the purser to Hayman's cabin. The purser informed the physician that Hayman was very sick and appeared to be at death's door. After examining Hayman, Griffin told the purser there was little he could do and that the man would likely die from his wounds before reaching New York.

A few more days passed and Griffin was once again disturbed by a knock on his door by the purser who requested to speak with him in private. Once inside Griffin's cabin, the purser told the doctor that Hayman had died. He also related tales of the passenger's career as a pirate and told the physician of the two treasure-filled chests currently stowed in his own cabin. He informed the doctor that Hayman's family was expected to meet him at the port in New York and were to take him and the treasure to some remote location in the interior of the state. The purser then proposed to Griffin that the two of them arrange to have the treasure secretly removed from the vessel and later divide it between them. Playing along with the purser's suggestion, Griffin agreed, but later that same evening he told his friend Compton about the visit and the offer. Griffin and Compton then concocted their own scheme to make off with the treasure.

Realizing the difficulty of unloading two extremely heavy chests at the busy port of New York, Griffin suggested instead that he and Compton remove the treasure during the ship's first stop at Newburyport in northeastern Massachusetts during a scheduled docking to unload some cargo.

When the ship landed at Newburyport, Griffin went into town on the pretense of sightseeing, but once there he arranged to rent a stout wagon and a pair of sturdy horses. Meanwhile, Compton waited for the purser to go into town and pick up some supplies. When the purser was safely away from the ship, Compton broke into his cabin, hacked open the treasure chests, removed all the coins, and placed them in canvas sacks that, in turn, he stowed in steamer trunks belonging to Griffin and him. Shortly afterward, Griffin arrived at the dock with the wagon, and, while no one was looking, the two men dragged the trunks from the boat and onto the platform. With the aid of four dockworkers who happened by, the men loaded the trunks onto the wagon and the two men drove away.

The two schemers planned to transport the gold to a selected location near Byfield a few miles inland and bury it. They would then return to their homes for a period of five years. When that time had elapsed and everyone had forgotten the incident, the pair intended to reunite and retrieve the gold.

Griffin and Compton drove the loaded wagon along the old Andover Road until they reached the Parker River that passed near Byfield. They stopped here, and, with great difficulty, pulled the trunks from the wagon and dragged them to a point near a prominent granite boulder. As Compton began to excavate a deep hole, Griffin chiseled the letter "A" onto the boulder to mark the site. When the hole was about four feet deep, the trunks were dumped into it, one on top of the other. The dirt was replaced and smoothed over, and the entire area was covered with local forest debris.

As the two men drove away in the wagon, a young boy named Howard Noyes lowered himself out of the tree where he'd watched the trunks being buried. Noyes immediately ran to his home where he related the incident to his family. Noyes's father did not believe the tale of buried treasure, gave the boy a whipping, and sent him to bed.

The following morning, Griffin and Compton abandoned the rented wagon and horses and booked passage on a coach for New York.

Young Howard Noyes continued to bedevil his family about the buried trunks. Eventually his father relented and allowed the boy to take him to the site near the bank of the Parker River. Though they easily located the boulder with the freshly scratched "A" on the side, Noyes was unable to identify the precise location where the trunks were buried.

Within a few days, the story of the buried treasure made the rounds of the region and people came from as far away as New York to search and dig, but the gold coins remained hidden.

Five years after burying the treasure, Griffin and Compton met but agreed to postpone their journey to Byfield to retrieve the treasure. Because the residents in the area were very aware of the story, the two men feared their presence might arouse undue curiosity. Time passed, and neither man was able to return to Byfield to unearth the great fortune that lay hidden near the river. By 1850, both were dead.

In 1923, Compton's great-granddaughter discovered his journal and read a detailed description of the theft of pirate Hayman's gold and its burial near Byfield. The great-granddaughter was so intrigued with the possibility of locating and recovering the fortune that she traveled to the small New England town.

Arriving at the picturesque community in northeastern Massachusetts, the great-granddaughter learned that many residents were still very familiar with the tale, which had been handed down through many generations. For several weeks, she supervised the excavation of dozens of holes near the granite boulder, but she found nothing and soon departed.

The great-granddaughter's visit to Byfield served to stimulate renewed interest in the cache, and soon others from the New England area arrived at the junction of the old Andover Road and the Parker River to search for the treasure. Nothing was found until 1932, and that amazing discovery was purely accidental.

During the spring of that year, Chauncey Braden, a laborer, was employed to dig a well for a Byfield resident. Braden often did odd jobs for Byfield residents and, though quite poor, had a reputation of being honest and dependable. The location of the well was near the granite boulder, now bearing a weathered but very readable "A" on its side.

The long, slow, and arduous labor of hand-digging the well took its toll on the middle-aged Braden and he stopped often to rest. A resident of Byfield, Orlin A. Arlin, passed by from time to time during his walks to check on the progress of the well and to chat with Braden.

One afternoon, Arlin passed by the unfinished well but Braden was nowhere in sight. When Arlin approached the excavation and peered within, he was surprised to discover several fragments of very old oak panels along with some metal hinges and leather straps.

No one in Byfield ever saw Braden again, but several months later Arlin stopped at a store a few miles to the north in the town of Salisbury where he heard a most remarkable story. The storekeeper related to Arlin how a common laborer had come up from Byfield, bought a load of goods, and paid with gold coins. The storekeeper showed the coins to Arlin who noticed they were all British and dated from 1794 to 1799. Though he tried for several weeks to locate Braden, Arlin was never able to find him.

From the time it was buried, hundreds of people have searched for the Byfield treasure, systematically excavating holes near the granite boulder. For years, none were successful, and then, apparently by pure chance, it was found by Chauncey Braden, a laborer, who instantly became a rich man.

But there may be more of the treasure in the original cache. Years later, when Arlin was reflecting on his experience, it occurred to him that when he peered into the excavation, he saw the remains of only one chest. There is a great possibility that the second one still lies a few feet below the surface near the granite boulder.

The Mysterious Marshfield Mansion

Located near the Atlantic Coast, Marshfield, Massachusetts, lies about three miles inland from the shore. Set peacefully adjacent to Highway 139, Marshfield is relatively undisturbed by the heavy traffic that moves up and down the much busier Highway 3, a popular route that carries Boston residents to and from the Cape Cod National Seashore and Martha's Vineyard. Today, Marshfield has a population of only about four thousand residents, and throughout its entire history it has remained a relatively small, quiet town.

During the late 1700s, Stuart Alton, Sr., a descendant of an early settler, a successful banker, and a dealer in properties, headed one of the most prominent Marshfield families. In 1789, Stuart Alton II, only twenty-one years old, was invited into the banking business with his father. His youthful enthusiasm, energy, and commitment to hard work provided many prosperous years. As the younger Alton matured into the banking business, he married his Marshfield sweetheart and eventually fathered three children.

By 1807, young Alton had completely taken over the family business. Eventually, he turned the bank's operation over to trusted employees, and, now a very wealthy man, he reveled in his new-found freedom and became involved in other pursuits. Eventually, Alton purchased a harpsichord and began taking music lessons, which brought him many hours of happiness and relaxation.

By 1810, Alton's skills on the harpsichord had improved and he decided to purchase an instrument of much higher quality than the one he currently owned. During a trip to Boston, he located a beautiful instrument that had been constructed by George Astor, the brother of John Jacob Astor. After examining the fine workmanship manifested on this handcrafted organ and hearing the dulcet tones coaxed forth from the ivory keys, Alton purchased the instrument and had it delivered to his home. Night after night, the banker played hymns and period musical pieces until he could scarcely sit upright on the stool. Aside from his wife and children, Alton loved the harpsichord more than anything.

During the War of 1812, Alton's wife, after visiting one of the children, was returning home on a small ship when it sank. Her body was never found. Alton was devastated, and on hearing the news, closed the lid to the harpsichord and swore never to play music again.

In search of some kind of distraction from his misery, Alton began fishing. Placing two or three fishing poles in a rowboat, he paddled two to three miles out into the ocean and fished alone until it was too dark to see.

Once when Alton was far from the shore on one of his fishing trips, he was captured by British sailors and imprisoned aboard their ship. After being held for nearly a month, he was finally released in Maine, and, weeks later, finally made his way back to Marshfield.

Between the loss of his wife and the trauma of imprisonment, Alton decided a change of scenery and routine was necessary. He moved from the long-time family home into an old mansion located near the center of town. Alton had long admired the old building and decided to devote some time and energy to establishing a special place for himself—a kind of retreat from the world. Intent on renovating the fine old structure, Alton spent thousands of dollars employing carpenters and masons. With the renovation completed, he found he desired to play the harpsichord once again and moved his fine instrument into his new residence.

One of the most dominant structures in the mansion was a huge fireplace, so large that a small man could nearly stand upright in it. Across from the fireplace, Alton placed his harpsichord, and, after building a bright fire, he played all night long in the wavering glow of the blaze.

By 1832, Alton completely retired from the bank and was regarded as one of the wealthiest men in the county. His children, grown with families of their own, lived nearby. As Christmas approached on the year of his retirement, Alton invited his children and grandchildren to come to the mansion to spend the holiday season with him.

On the final evening of the holiday gathering, Alton assembled his family in the large living room by the fire and told them he would like to play the harpsichord for them. The children were so impressed with their father's playing that they encouraged him to make the Christmas gathering an annual affair.

More time passed, and Alton began composing most of his music. For hours he would sit at the harpsichord and play, and Marshfield residents often stood outside his window and listened to the beautiful music.

In autumn 1851, Alton stumbled and fell from the mansion's high front porch and received a serious injury. In spite of the handicap, he hosted once again the family Christmas gathering. Following the feasting and conversation, Alton invited his family into the large fireplace room and played for them his latest compositions. During the last piece, however, Alton grabbed his chest and collapsed onto the floor. Moments later, Stuart Alton II was dead.

Three days later, Alton was buried, and on the Monday of the following week, family and friends gathered at the mansion for the reading of his will. Anticipations ran high, for at the time of his death Alton was believed to be an incredibly wealthy man. In his declining years, he spent very little money, and his fortune was estimated to be worth well over a million dollars—an impressive sum of money at the time.

Surprisingly, the harpsichord, the fireplace, and the remaining furnishings found on the premises were virtually the only items listed in the will. Stunned by the fact that no money was mentioned, the relatives quickly examined Alton's bank account only to discover it contained a mere $12,000! Bank records revealed that for the past twenty years, Alton made modest yet consistent withdrawals in the form of ten and twenty dollar gold pieces. What he did with the money, no one could guess.

Since the harpsichord had been mentioned prominently in the will, it was immediately disassembled to see if any money was hidden within, but none was there. They also inspected the huge fireplace, but nothing out of the ordinary could be found.

What became of Stuart Alton's fortune was a mystery.

About one year following Alton's death, one of his sons moved into the mansion, where he lived with his family for the rest of his life. In 1896, the son died, and his daughter, Lucy, took over the residence.

Lucy, more than any of the other children, remained fascinated with her grandfather's wealth, and she often spent hours searching about the house. For years, she continued to believe that the clue to finding the treasure was somehow associated with the harpsichord. Time and again she inspected the fine instrument, and time and again she closely examined Alton's own musical compositions hoping to find some key. Alas, there were none.

By the end of the Civil War, Lucy Alton was the only member of the once prominent family left alive. At war's end, she still resided in the mansion, now playing her grandfather's harpsichord each night before retiring.

One evening, after playing some of her grandfather's compositions, Lucy Alton closed the lid to the instrument and climbed the stairs to her bedroom. She soon fell asleep, and that night she had a strange dream.

In the dream, a wispy image of an old man who she had never seen before but knew it had to be her grandfather, appeared. The image quietly and confidently seated itself at the harpsichord and began playing the same music Lucy had performed earlier that evening. Behind the image, a fire burned in the large fireplace.

Finally, the image closed the harpsichord, rose from the stool, and walked over to stand near the warm hearth. After a moment, the apparition retrieved a poker from the side of the fireplace, walked into the flames, and turned to look at something in the interior on the left side. Presently, the image, raising the poker, tapped at several of the bricks. Then, the image slowly faded away and Lucy Alton awoke.

Lying in bed wondering about the dream's significance, Lucy heard the faint sound of music coming from downstairs. As she listened, the music grew louder, and she recognized it as that of her grandfather. When she went to investigate, the music stopped, and the harpsichord was closed up tightly.

The next morning, Lucy Alton went to the fireplace, and, after moving aside the hot coals from the previous night's blaze, examined it closely, particularly the left inside wall. Uncertain of what she was looking for, she decided to summon a stonemason.

Later that same day, James Hamilton, a stone worker, arrived, and Lucy Alton asked him to inspect the fireplace for anything out of the ordinary. Having no idea what the old woman meant,

Hamilton entered the large fireplace and began examining the rock and masonry closely. Several minutes later, he told Lucy that he had discovered a large brick that appeared to have been cemented into the structure at the time it was originally constructed, removed sometime later, and then remortared into place. Lucy asked him to remove the brick, and within thirty minutes he had dislodged it from its place.

When Lucy entered the fireplace she peered into the opening and discovered a dark space several inches wide. Reaching into the cavity, her fingers probed about but encountered nothing. She asked Hamilton to remove more bricks.

Three additional bricks were knocked out, exposing more of the dark cavity. Leaning as far as he could into the space, Hamilton extended his arm downward as far as he was able and told Lucy he felt something. After several minutes of struggling, Hamilton turned to Lucy and told her he thought he could feel coins. Moments later, he withdrew a twenty dollar gold piece! Several more attempts produced a number of ten and twenty dollar gold coins. Smiling widely, Lucy Alton suddenly realized she had discovered her grandfather's long lost treasure!

For reasons no one was ever able to discern, Stuart Alton apparently decided to employ the large, custom-made fireplace as a bizarre receptacle for his fortune that he had converted into gold coins.

It may be that the old man was going to explain his actions to his children that Christmas night when he suddenly died at the harpsichord.

However, with the help of a strange dream and a bit of luck, the treasure was eventually discovered.

The Maynard Treasure

Boston, with its busy docks, booming businesses, loud taverns, and around-the-clock social life, had grown far too hectic for many conservative residents during the late seventeenth and early eighteenth centuries. A number of these Bostonians packed up and migrated in search of less populated regions where they could establish farms and live a relatively peaceful and quiet life. In this way, the town of Maynard, about twenty miles east of downtown Boston, became established.

Like so many others who sought the solitude of the eastern Massachusetts interior, Thomas Smith brought his family to Maynard, constructed a suitable log cabin, and bent to the task of preparing his fields for crops. The Smith farm was located near the Assabet River, so fresh water was plentiful. Deer and other game populated the woods, and the area streams were fished and trapped for fur-bearing mammals. Life in Maynard was good for the Smith family, and when the crops came up the next season, it would be even better.

In 1720, before Smith had been living a full year on his newly acquired land, an unusual-looking group of six men arrived at his cabin. They came on foot, and each of them was garbed in clothes more fitting for a life at sea. Three men carried bulky packs, and they all pushed and pulled three heavily laden handcarts. Negotiating the handcarts down the poor road was clearly difficult for them, and the men appeared quite weary from the chore.

After calling farmer Smith from the field, the newcomers asked politely if they could stay in his barn for a few days and rest from their journey. At first, Smith feared that if he refused the men would grow hostile, but as he spoke with them he found them to be quite friendly and courteous. They even offered to help Smith with his chores.

That evening, Smith's wife fed the visitors a hearty meal, and the men ate, as if famished. When the strangers finally retired to the barn for the night, Mrs. Smith noted that one had left a gold coin under one of the plates. Inspecting it closely, farmer Smith saw that it was a Spanish coin—a piece-of-eight—and he wondered how his visitors had acquired it.

Early the following morning when Smith went to work in his fields, he passed by the barn and noticed that his visitors were awake and outside. All six, laughing and conversing, were stationed along one side of the barn and were throwing objects at the swallows that darted in and out among the rafters. After a few minutes of watching this target practice, Smith was suddenly stunned to discover that his guests hurled pieces-of-eight at the birds! Always one to mind his own business, Smith merely nodded a greeting and went about his daily tasks. On witnessing the carefree manner in which the strangers tossed around precious gold coins, however, Smith began wondering what had actually been transported on the handcarts.

For nearly a week, the visitors remained in the barn, coming out occasionally to help Smith, to eat their meals, or simply to engage in conversation with their hosts. The group remained quite congenial, and the Smiths eventually grew comfortable with their presence.

One morning, two of the visitors appeared at the cabin's back door and asked Mrs. Smith if she could spare any old clothing and rags. After receiving an armload of cloth scraps, the men carried them to the barn and spent the remainder of the day fashioning sacks.

The next morning, the same two men appeared once again at the cabin and asked to borrow some shovels and picks. About an hour later, the entire group was seen pulling and pushing their handcarts along a crude trail that led into the woods. Two carried the cloth sacks and digging tools.

Sometime later that afternoon when Thomas Smith came in from the fields, he encountered his visitors returning along the forest trail. They were cheerful as they hiked along the trail singing, and when they saw the farmer they waved a greeting. Smith noted fresh dirt clinging to the tips of the shovels. He also observed that the handcarts appeared much lighter than they seemed on the day the men arrived.

The following morning, the six men appeared once again at the Smith cabin. This time, they thanked Thomas Smith and his wife for their hospitality and, just before leaving, presented them with a bag of coins. After the men had disappeared down the road, Smith opened the sack to find ten pieces-of-eight!

After Smith's guests departed, several neighbors arrived at the farm to inquire about the recent visitors. Smith related nothing at all about the pieces-of-eight, and merely said the men only were resting up from a journey. Several of the farmer's neighbors commented that the strangers appeared to be dressed like pirates and wondered aloud why they had come to Maynard.

About eighteen months later, Thomas Smith received a letter from Boston. Reading the crude script, the farmer discovered the missive had been written by one of the six men who had stayed at his farm. The letter, already two weeks old, explained that the man and his companions had been caught in the act of piracy and were awaiting execution at the Boston jail. The writer of the letter implored Smith to dig up a portion of the treasure they placed in the cloth sacks and buried on his farm and bring it to Boston so that it could be offered in exchange for their lives.

At that moment, Smith realized his suspicions were correct—that a treasure, undoubtedly consisting, at least in part, of gold pieces-of-eight, had indeed been interred somewhere nearby in the woods.

Having absolutely no idea where the treasure could possibly have been buried, Smith determined to travel to Boston and meet with the prisoners in order to obtain the appropriate information.

Several days passed since important farm chores needed attention, but finally Smith loaded his wagon, hitched up his team, bade his wife goodbye, and made the long journey into Boston.

Arriving at the jail, Thomas Smith learned that the six men, all well-known pirates, had been hanged the previous day for their crimes.

On the day following his return to the farm, Smith and his wife spent may hours walking in the woods where they suspected the pirates had buried the treasure but found no clues whatsoever. They searched off and on for many years, but the location of the buried pirate treasure in Maynard has always remained a mystery.

Hog Island's Coin Cave

Hog Island, Massachusetts, is located in the relatively protected Atlantic waters along the state's northeastern shore. Lying just south of the Castle Neck peninsula and not far from the coastal town of Gloucester, Hog Island has seen only sparse settlement and visitation during the past three hundred years.

In 1813, Englishman John Wilson Breed purchased Hog Island, located at the extreme northwestern edge of Essex Bay and at the time called Suzanna Island. Here, Breed constructed an elaborately grand mansion with many rooms. Employing two full-time gardeners, the Englishman supervised the landscaping of the grounds to include a number of flower and herb beds, along with a variety of imported trees and shrubs.

Breed had been a successful merchant in England and over the years, had branched out into exporting goods from Europe to the growing cities along the American coast. In time, Breed became a wealthy man by anyone's standards and eventually decided he had made all of the money he cared to make. Seeking a simpler lifestyle and anxious to spend more time with his family, he sold his British enterprises and retired to Boston.

After visiting Hog Island one summer about a year-and-a-half after moving to Boston, Breed was impressed with the somewhat remote and isolated location. Deciding that this quiet sanctuary was to his liking, he purchased Hog Island and decided to move onto it at the earliest opportunity.

During his time as a businessman in England, Breed never developed a trust in banks and never deposited so much as a single pence in any of them. He converted all of his money to gold and silver coins and kept them hidden in a number of secret locations.

When Breed moved to Massachusetts, he carried his fortune in several trunks that were kept under constant heavy guard. After settling in Boston, Breed searched for and eventually found a new location to hide his wealth. After loading his heavy coin-filled trunks onto a stout wagon, the Englishman drove about three miles west of town and buried them in the woods. Though his wife and children begged him to disclose the secret location of his cache, he never told them.

Following his purchase of Hog Island, Breed spent many enjoyable hours overseeing the construction of his mansion, walking around his property, exploring the hills and shorelines, and reveling in the fresh and invigorating sea breezes that blew in from the Atlantic Ocean. Breed noted that many caves dotted his island, and he delighted in exploring them.

During a visit to nearby Gloucester to purchase some supplies, Breed met a curious Indian who went by the name of Gossum. Elderly and slightly crippled, Gossum rarely spoke other than to mutter a few incoherent sounds. Gloucester citizens regarded Gossum as harmless, and they often provided him with table scraps. At night, the Indian slept under the front porch of a hardware store.

On the day Breed arrived in Gloucester, Gossum was warming himself in the afternoon sun on the west side of a building. As the Englishman struggled with a particularly heavy load, Gossum rose and offered to help. For the next several minutes, the Indian hauled Breed's supplies from the store and packed them into the wagon.

With the purchases loaded, the Englishman pulled a coin from his pocket and offered it to the Indian. Gossum merely stared at it curiously for a moment and walked away. A clerk in the hardware store who was watching from the door explained to Breed that Gossum did not understand the use or value of money. Tapping the side of his head with his index finger, the clerk told Breed that the Indian was a bit simple.

Impressed with Gossum's initiative, however, Breed asked the Indian to come to Hog Island and work for him. The Indian agreed, and the two rode off in the wagon toward the dock where the Englishman's boat was tied.

Several weeks later, Breed told his wife that he had found a perfect hiding location for his fortune. It was a cave, he explained, located less than a quarter of a mile from the house, but one that offered protection and concealment for his gold and silver. After dinner, he said, he and Gossum would transport the treasure to the cave and bury it. Though Mrs. Breed begged her husband to reveal the cave's location, he would not do so.

After concealing the chests in the cave, Breed and Gossum were returning to the house when the Indian pointed to another cave not far from the one where the treasure was buried. The Indian indicated that he preferred to live there.

Breed acceded to Gossum's wish, and during the next few days, the two men hauled a pallet, a lantern, firewood, and several blankets to the cave.

Life was good on Hog Island, both for the Breed family and for Gossum. For thirty-three years, John Wilson Breed devoted himself to his wife, children, grandchildren, and the grounds. He expanded his flower beds, planted more shrubs, and took daily walks along several of the island's trails.

In time, Breed's children grew up, went off to school, married, and moved to towns on the mainland. They and their own children returned several times each year to Hog Island for family reunions and picnics. Sometimes, one or another of his children asked about the location of Breed's buried treasure, but the old man remained evasive and always quickly changed the subject.

Gossum was Breed's constant companion during those years, and together the two men explored the island and fished the waters of the bay. From time to time, Breed found it necessary to add to or withdraw coins from his cache. On those occasions, he summoned Gossum, and the two men went to the secret cave and dug up one of the trunks.

On several occasions, Breed offered Gossum money, but each time the Indian refused it. The Englishman eventually came to understand the Indian was simply unconcerned about such things. In 1846, John Wilson Breed suffered a heart attack and died instantly. Enlisting Gossum's help, Breed's wife buried the Englishman on the property. The service was attended by all of Breed's children and grandchildren along with several dignitaries and merchants from Gloucester and nearby Ipswich.

The Breed offspring remained at the Hog Island mansion for several days following the funeral to divide some of their father's belongings and to make arrangements for his ongoing business affairs. While discussing these things, the conversation eventually turned to the topic of Breed's buried wealth. Aware that Gossum was the only person other than their father who knew the treasure's location, they determined to have the Indian direct them to it on the morrow.

The next morning, several family members searched for the Indian's cave. Because none of them had ever visited the odd residence before, it was several hours before they finally located it. Gossum was gone!

Inside the cave, they found the still warm embers of a fire from the previous night, a pallet, and a few worn blankets, but the Indian was nowhere.

For two days, the Breed children searched the entire island but found no trace of Gossum whatsoever. They presumed the Indian departed for the shore after Breed's death, but none of the boats was missing, and they had no idea how he could have negotiated the waters between the island and the mainland.

Knowing only that their father's treasure was hidden in a cave, the Breed children undertook a systematic search of the island that lasted for two weeks. To their dismay, however, they discovered that Hog Island contained dozens, if not hundreds, of caves, many of which were capable of accommodating several wooden trunks.

For days, they dug into scores of these caves, only to find nothing. Eventually, the need to return to their respective homes and businesses forced an end to the search, but on several occasions each year, they returned to Hog Island and renewed their quest for their father's hidden treasure.

The hunt for John Wilson Breed's lost fortune continued off and on for the next ten years but with no success. Eventually, the family members tired of the hunt and moved on to other diversions.

Some researchers acquainted with the tale of Breed's lost treasure argue that the faithful Gossum absconded with it. Close attention to the details of the history of the Englishman's fortune, however, suggest that this is unlikely. On several occasions, Gossum refused money when it was offered to him, and, according to those who were acquainted with him, the Indian knew nothing about the value of such things. During the thirty-three years he lived on Hog Island, Gossum had ample opportunity to spirit away all or portions of Breed's fortune. The apparent fact is Gossum remained entirely loyal to his employer. When Breed died, the Indian had no reason to remain, and so he simply departed. It is further unlikely that he would have been able to flee with the heavy chests in which Breed kept his gold and silver coins.

Others who have studied this fascinating tale are convinced that Breed's treasure is still hidden somewhere in an island cave. Evidence of this surfaced during the 1950s.

In 1956, two Gloucester residents sailed to Hog Island to spend the day exploring it. During a hike around the eastern part of the island, they came upon a shallow cave. As they neared the cave, it began to rain, so the two friends scrambled inside the opening to wait out the storm.

Approximately one hour later, the rain subsided, the clouds parted, and sunshine broke through. The two men stepped out of the cave and were about to return to their boat when one of them spotted a shiny object in the mud at their feet. Examining the source of the reflection, they discovered a gold coin with a mint date of 1819. Digging through the moist soil, they found three more coins. Though they searched for another hour in the dirt and rubble just outside the cave opening, they found nothing more.

After returning to Gloucester and announcing their discovery, the two friends were told the story of John Wilson Breed's long-lost treasure. Convinced they had chanced upon Breed's hiding place, the two men made plans to return to Hog Island at the first opportunity.

Commitments to jobs and families, however, kept the two from returning to the island for several weeks, but finally they were able to make the short boat trip from Gloucester to Essex Bay.

After landing on the eastern side of Hog Island, the two friends disagreed over which trail they had taken during their earlier visit. Several forays along different routes into the interior of the island only got them lost and disoriented. Though they encountered several caves, none of them was the one in which they had waited out the rainstorm weeks earlier.

The two friends searched until dusk and then headed back to Gloucester.

Subsequent return trips to Hog Island over the next few years yielded similar results—the cave where they found the gold coins could not be found. Others who learned of their discovery came to search the island and, though a number of caves were located, subsequent excavations yielded no treasure.

Somewhere within a quarter mile of the old Breed mansion lies a buried fortune. The gold and silver coins, packed into at least four wooden trunks, are likely buried in a shallow cave. John Wilson Breed was far too clever to have hidden his treasure in a cave that was close to a trail for fear that it would be discovered by others.

Will Sexton, a professional treasure hunter, has offered an explanation relative to why the Breed treasure has been so difficult to locate. Sexton claims that Breed knew anyone searching for a cave would have an easy time finding it. With the help of Gossum, suggests Sexton, Breed stacked rocks in front of the cave's opening so that it would appear much like any other part of the landscape. With that theory, Sexton is planning a renewed search for the long-lost treasure of John Wilson Breed.

Treasure in the Grave

Alden Culver only wanted to be a farmer and live a quiet and peaceful life with his wife and daughter near the small community of West Chesterfield, Massachusetts. In spite of his wishes, Culver often found himself defending his farm and home against attacking Indians, killing several in the process. Culver was so successful in defending his property that he soon earned an unwanted reputation as a fierce Indian fighter. To many white settlers in the region, he was a hero, but to the Indians, he was regarded as a hated foe and one on whom they swore revenge.

During the early part of the nineteenth century, skirmishes between white settlers and the Indians in western Massachusetts were frequent and sometimes quite bloody. Newly arriving settlers often intruded into lands that were long the traditional hunting domain of the natives. The subsequent establishment of cattle herds, homes, and small communities led to a scarcity of wild game and a displacement of the Indians who, in turn, grew more and more hostile to the newcomers.

Sometimes alone, and sometimes in the company of others, Culver fought bravely and fiercely against small bands of raiders intent on burning his home, stealing his cattle, and ultimately driving him, along with other whites, out of the area.

In addition to his standing as an able Indian fighter, Culver was a shrewd businessman who regularly earned respectable profits from the sale of his livestock and feed. Over the years, he amassed an impressive fortune in gold and silver coins that he kept locked in an iron box hidden somewhere in the woods not far from his house. The key to the box always hung from Culver's belt.

Over the years, Culver suffered numerous wounds from his frequent, hostile encounters with Indians. The pain and severity of the many injuries, according to Culver's neighbors, eventually caused the respected farmer to become insane. As he grew older, Culver was often spotted wandering aimlessly along roads and in the woods near his farm, mumbling to himself and claiming he was being pursued by Indians. Each time he was found, the man was returned to the care of his wife and daughter.

In time, Culver's wife passed away, and his daughter assumed the responsibility of seeing to the needs of her father who was growing more feeble with each passing month.

In spite of his fame as an Indian fighter, Culver counted among his favored companions a friendly Indian named Moosuk. Moosuk lived peacefully among the whites, often worked for them, and on occasion attempted to negotiate among them and the warring nearby tribes.

One day, Moosuk encountered Culver walking in the woods near his farm, carrying a shovel, and babbling incoherently. When Culver began excavating a hole, Moosuk asked him what he was doing.

Culver explained to his friend that he was digging his own grave and that he didn't expect to live much longer. He told Moosuk that he had a premonition that he would be killed by Indians before the next full moon.

When Culver had finished with the hole, he exacted a promise from Moosuk that, on his death, the Indian would bury him in this spot along with his iron box full of coins. The Indian agreed, and Culver took his friend deeper into the woods and showed him where the fortune was hidden.

The next day, Culver told his daughter about the premonition and his desire to be buried in the woods along with his iron box. After explaining his plans, he removed the key from his belt and presented it to her. Believing her father had merely lapsed into one of his now common demented ramblings, she accepted the key, nodded, and returned to her chores.

Culver's premonition of death came true, for two days before the moon was at its fullest, he was ambushed by Indians along the road to West Chesterfield and killed. When Moosuk found him the following day, he carried the farmer to the grave, retrieved the box of coins from its hiding place, laid it alongside the body, and filled the hole.

Walking several yards to a large, flat rock, Moosuk carved the name "Alden Culver" into it and added the year. Following this, he went to Alden's house and informed the daughter of her father's death and burial. Though the daughter made no attempt to excavate the grave and retrieve the iron box of coins, she nevertheless always carried the key with her everywhere she went.

Several years later, Culver's daughter died and Moosuk buried her in the woods beside her father. As he laid her carefully into the grave, the Indian noticed the key attached to a belt she wore. Having little knowledge of or concern for the value or use of money, Moosuk left the key alone. On a second large, flat rock not far from the one he had carved Culver's name years earlier, he now carved the daughter's name and the year of her death.

More time passed, and Moosuk, now aged and somewhat feeble, was fed and cared for by Simon James, a Northampton merchant. Each day, the old Indian grew weaker, and it was apparent he would soon die.

One evening when James brought food to the tiny room where Moosuk stayed, the old Indian pulled him close and told him the story of Alden Culver, the iron box filled with gold and silver coins, and the key. Fascinated, James listened intently to the Indian's tale. When the storekeeper pressed the Indian for details and landmarks, Moosuk fell back on the bed, too weak to continue. Later that night, Moosuk died.

A few weeks following Moosuk's death, James traveled to the old Culver farm and searched for several days throughout the surrounding woods for the stone markers. Since the Indian provided no directions or landmarks relative to the location of the graves, James was forced to explore a large tract of woods. The merchant was ill-suited for the task, and eventually the thick woods, dense briars, and lack of success discouraged him. He eventually returned to Northampton and never again tried to locate Culver's grave.

In 1936, nearly one hundred years following Alden Culver's death, a Chesterfield school teacher related some history and folklore of the region to a group of fifth graders. After telling them the story of Culver's lost treasure, one of the boys excitedly informed the teacher that he actually had seen the names of Culver and his daughter inscribed on rocks located on his father's farm.

Returning home later that afternoon, the youth told the Culver tale to his father, and they, along with the school teacher and several neighbors, went into the woods in search of the stones, which were easily located.

Because the tale of Culver's buried treasure contained no information whatsoever with regard to the actual location of the graves relative to the stones, no one knew in which direction to search. A number of holes were excavated near the inscribed stones and several more a short distance away, but nothing was found.

Over the years, the land's owner excavated at least two hundred more holes in the area, but found nothing.

Today, with modern metal detection equipment, experts claim finding the coin-filled chest would be a simple matter. Unfortunately, no one still living in the area recalls the exact location of the inscribed stones.

In 1976, a group of birdwatchers from Springfield, Massachusetts, hiked several miles along the banks of the Westfield River in a segment of woods located in Hampshire County. Carrying binoculars, field guides, and notebooks, the birders were conducting a census of the different kinds of avifauna found in the region. Days later, following the final tally, a box filled with the census data, several journals, and related materials was given to the library at Springfield.

In 1985, while examining data on certain migratory birds, a researcher encountered the box of materials. While perusing the journals and notebooks for pertinent information, the researcher encountered a curious entry in one of them.

The writer, who has never been identified, mentioned stopping for a short break near "two flat stones that bore inscriptions." The names on the stones, according to the journal, were Culver. Believing they were headstones, the birdwatcher remained only a few minutes and left. The journal contained no locational information pertinent to the inscribed stones but verified the fact that the markers still exist.

And somewhere not far away under a few feet of soil lies Alden Culver's iron box filled with gold and silver coins.

Chappaquiddick's Blue Rock Treasure

On the western edge of Chappaquiddick Island lies Cape Poge, a curled and sandy extension of the isle that faces Nantucket Sound. In the years before advanced high-tech, ultra-sensitive navigation instruments, the Cape Poge Lighthouse warned approaching vessels of the shallow shoals. Not far from this lighthouse and scattered along a stretch of beach lie several rocks, some of which could be classified as boulders.

James Roland Cooke, an aged, reclusive man, farmed a portion of Chappaquiddick Island near Cape Poge. Sailing his skiff to the mainland only rarely to conduct business and purchase supplies, Cooke preferred the solitude and quiet of the island and the company of his cattle. Two or three times each year, Cooke made arrangements for the delivery of some of his cattle to Falmouth where they would be auctioned for a good price.

The few men who knew Cooke regarded him as daft. He spent too much time alone on the island with his cattle, they told one another, attributing Cooke's growing senility to his solitude.

One day around sundown in 1824, Cooke was walking along a portion of the sandy neck that forms part of Cape Poge in search of several head of lost cattle. As he looked for his livestock, he suddenly heard the sound of conversation coming across the open water on the Atlantic Ocean side. Pausing, Cooke peered out into the blue waters toward the north and eventually spotted a small craft—a row boat—approaching the shore. Curious about the identity of the newcomers, Cooke found a hiding place behind a nearby patch of tall grass on a low bank overlooking the beach.

As the old man watched, the rowboat struck the shore and five men jumped out, seized the gunwales, and pulled the boat several feet up onto the sands. Regarding the newcomers, Cooke determined by their dress that they were pirates, though he could find no sign of a ship anchored in the ocean as far as he could see.

Presently, four of the men climbed back into the boat and, with great difficulty, removed a heavy wooden chest and set it on the beach. This done, the fifth man, apparently the leader, reached into the craft and pulled out three shovels. Standing next to the rowboat, he began looking around the beach as if searching for something. He pointed to a large boulder about forty yards away and just above the high tide level. After voicing a command to his four companions, the leader, carrying the shovels, started walking toward the large rock. The other four lifted the chest and, laboring under the great weight, followed the other toward the boulder.

As Cooke observed the activity on the beach, he noticed that the boulder toward which the newcomers were headed had a bluish tint in the fading sunlight.

On reaching the boulder, the leader directed the others to begin excavating a deep hole. As he stood and watched, the other four took turns digging until a cavity approximately six feet deep had been dug. As the pirates dug, Cooke gazed in open-eyed wonder at the chest and tried to imagine the amount and kind of treasure it contained.

Carefully, the large wooden chest was lowered into the hole. Then, two of the men reached for the shovels to begin refilling the hole when the leader and one of the others pulled pistols from their sashes and shot and killed their comrades. They threw the three dead men into the excavation and quickly filled it in.

After smoothing over the freshly turned sand, the two surviving members of the expedition carried the shovels back to the boat and pushed the craft into the water. With each of the men taking an oar, they rowed the boat away from the cape and north toward the mainland.

Farmer Cooke waited until the pirates were completely out of sight before rising from his place of hiding. Frightened that they might suddenly decide to return, Cooke turned and fled back in the direction from which he had come. On arriving at his cabin, he entered it, boarded up the door, and cowered in fright in one corner for the rest of the night.

When dawn finally arrived and sunlight streaked across Chappaquiddick Island through the parting fog, Cooke came out of his house. For several minutes, he debated with himself about whether or not he should return to Cape Poge and renew his search for his missing cattle. Finally, he argued that it was necessary to find the animals and return them to their pens.

As Cooke passed the patch of grass where he had watched the events of the previous evening, he considered walking to the place where the chest was buried and digging it up. As he scanned the beach, he was surprised to notice there were several large boulders, and at first he was not entirely certain which one was near the treasure chest. He soon spotted the blue rock, recognized it as the one, and approached it.

After examining the beach near the boulder, Cooke found where the sand had been disturbed. Along with a freshly dug hole, there were also several sets of footprints. About two hours later, Cooke located his missing cattle and herded them back to the pens. During the night, Cooke decided to report the pirate incident to the authorities, so he launched his skiff and set a course for Falmouth to seek out a constable.

On landing in Falmouth, Cooke was unable to locate the constable and instead approached several dockworkers and told them his story. Cooke was well known to the workers, and since all of them considered the old man quite eccentric, if not entirely crazy, they laughed at his tale and sent him on his way. After several hours of trying to find someone to believe his story, Cooke, dejected, finally returned to Chappaquiddick Island.

Several days later, Cooke, carrying a shovel and harboring hopes of finding a great treasure, returned to the beach where the wooden chest was buried. After identifying the blue rock, he approached it and looked for signs of the fresh excavation. Unfortunately, strong winds from the night before had smoothed out the beach sands, and Cooke could not relocate the exact burial site.

Excitedly, he dug several holes, but after an hour of hard work he found nothing and grew too tired to continue. Subsequent trips to the this part of the beach over the next few weeks failed to uncover the buried treasure chest. Cooke, an old man, passed away only a few months later without ever finding the treasure.

It is believed by many who have researched this tale that the chest Cooke saw buried near the blue rock did indeed contain a pirate treasure.

If the mysterious blue rock on Cape Poge could ever be positively identified, it is possible that this chest and its contents, along with the skeletons of three pirates, would be found.

The Stash on Martha's Vineyard

Based on the evidence, hundreds, perhaps thousands, of treasures have been lost or hidden in New England during the past three centuries. Many of these tales turn out to be just stories and nothing more, merely fanciful renderings of an imagined event designed to entertain or trick the gullible. In an impressively large number of cases of lost mines and hidden treasures, however, the historical documentation quite often verifies some or all elements of the tale, thereby providing evidence—and hope—that the treasure still lies unrecovered and awaiting some patient and persistent searcher.

Sometime during the American Revolution from 1775 to 1783, a French galleon transporting supplies and a large wooden chest filled with gold coins ran atop a shoal immediately south of Martha's Vineyard, a popular island in the Atlantic Ocean located only four miles from the Massachusetts mainland. Vineyard Sound separates Martha's Vineyard from the Elizabeth Islands chain lying just to the northwest, and Nantucket Sound provides several miles of open water between the island and the Massachusetts coast lying to the northeast. The collision with the obstruction caused two serious problems for the officers and crew: The ship was hopelessly stuck; the hull damaged beyond repair.

Unknown to all but a few people, the vessel was transporting a great sum of money in the form of gold coins to be used as part of the payroll for French soldiers stationed in America. The galleon's officers, realizing the ship was hopelessly grounded, decided to abandon it, make their way to the coast, and await rescue. In the meantime, they needed to find a hiding place for the gold.

The Frenchmen placed only the most elementary supplies necessary for survival into the four rowboats and made preparations to cross the sound to the Massachusetts shore near Hyannis, a small settlement. Just before abandoning the ship, the captain ordered the chest filled with gold placed in one of the boats. Together, the four crafts rowed toward the southern shore of Martha's Vineyard.

After landing, the captain ordered several crewmen to carry the treasure chest to a point high on the beach near a large pond. Here, a relatively shallow hole was quickly excavated and the chest lowered into it. The captain informed the seamen that, once a rescue was started, they would return for the chest and deliver it to its intended destination.

Minutes later, all four boats rowed away from the island across Nantucket Sound toward the mainland. For reasons lost to history, the French never returned for the treasure chest.

One day in 1920, nearly a century-and-a-half following the burial of the chest on Martha's Vineyard, an island resident was riding horseback along the southern beach near a group of lakes called the Great Ponds when he made an amazing discovery. As he trotted his mare along a trail, the animal's left foreleg suddenly plunged into a small, unseen hole in the sand, causing the rider to spill.

After determining the animal was uninjured, the rider inspected the hole. Using only his hands, he scraped away several inches of sand to reveal the top of a wooden trunk. The trunk was apparently very old, and the wood was quite rotten. The partially decomposed lid of the buried trunk had collapsed inward, causing some of the surface sand to seep into the structure and thus creating the small hole.

Reaching into the trunk, the rider withdrew a handful of gold coins, all of French origin and possessing 1773 mint dates. One version of this tale has the finder informing federal authorities of his discovery. The government, according to the story, took possession of the gold and paid the finder a handsome reward. Research into this account found no evidence whatsoever of a government seizure of the treasure or payment of a reward.

The second version of the tale, and likely the true one, has the finder converting the gold to cash and retiring wealthy on Martha's Vineyard. The finder's descendants, all members of a wealthy and prominent family, reside on the island today, and they attribute their fortune to their ancestor's discovery of the gold-filled treasure chest.

CONNECTICUT

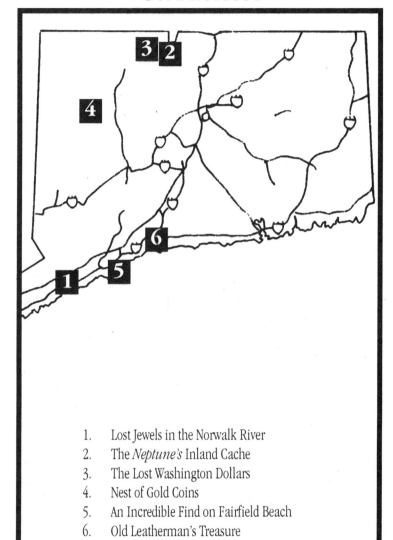

Lost Jewels in the Norwalk River

As a result of human error, a passenger train carrying more than $250,000 in jewelry and precious stones plunged into the Norwalk River in 1853. In the days following the accident, the channel was cleared of the wreckage, but the two wooden chests containing the gold, silver, diamonds, opals, pearls, emeralds, and rubies were never found.

Thaddeus Birke, a well-known and highly successful importer, was a passenger on the New Haven Railroad train as it sped along its route on the morning of May 6, 1853. Birke specialized in importing fine jewels and precious stones into the United States and also operated a highly profitable business in New York City. An Englishman, Birke enjoyed a stellar reputation among internationally known jewelers and European distributors. Wealthy businessmen and customers in the United States, France, Belgium, England, and Holland often sought his advice and expertise as it related to opening new markets in America.

As Birke's fame and fortune grew, he became the darling of American high society and was often invited to magnificent parties and dinners at the homes of the wealthy and famous in Connecticut, New York, and Massachusetts.

One afternoon, Birke received an engraved invitation to one such fancy formal gathering at the home of Boston millionaire Nigel Massey. Massey, the owner of a large and successful international shipping company, had, in addition to Birke, invited a number of of Boston's upper social echelon. At the party, Birke was expected to display some his finest merchandise.

Birke, seizing the opportunity to reap a tremendous profit, spent several days selecting the finest of his most recent imports. He carefully packed his merchandise, which included diamonds ranging up to thirty carats, emeralds of the highest quality, opals, rubies, pearls, and a wide variety of exquisitely crafted jewelry and ornaments fashioned from the purest gold and silver into two stout wooden chests. Birke's inventory was estimated to be worth just over $250,000.

Early on the morning of May 6, Birke supervised the loading of the two treasure-filled trunks onto the leading passenger car of the New Haven Railroad train. Birke made reservations for several first-class seats to accommodate himself and the trunks. A cautious man, Birke did not care to have his valuable shipment transported in the freight car so far away from his careful attention. As the train slowly pulled out of the New York station, Birke rode with each of his arms draped protectively across the tops of the chests.

As the train steamed along toward Boston, Birke contented himself with watching the passing scenery. From the window on the passenger car's right side, he observed fishermen hauling in nets filled with the day's first catch from the waters of Long Island Sound. Sailboats out on the water caught the wind and fairly skimmed across the surface, almost keeping pace with the train.

As the train passed through the quiet towns of Larchmont and Rye along a route that roughly coincides with present-day Highway 1, the passenger car's steady rumbling and rhythmic motion gradually lulled Birke to sleep in the early morning hours.

As the train approached the town of Stamford, Connecticut, around ten o'clock, the steamship *Pacific* was nearing the estuary that led to the Norwalk Harbor. From his pilot house, the vessel's captain could see up ahead the railroad bridge that crossed the wide channel at a point where the estuary narrowed to the river's mouth.

In a control tower adjacent to the drawbridge, the operator recognized the oncoming cargo vessel and began making preparations to open the bridge and allow passage. After the signal used to alert oncoming trains was raised, the operator activated the mechanism that opened the huge drawbridge.

The Norwalk River Railroad Bridge was not the traditional type of drawbridge that parted in the middle with the two separated sections lifted to sharp angles. Instead, the long, middle section of this bridge rotated to a position parallel to the river's current, thus leaving sufficient room for the passage of ocean-going ships.

Once the bridge was fully opened and the channel passable, the bridge operator waved the *Pacific* on through. As the operator smoked a cigarette and watched, the ship passed slowly upriver.

After adjusting the mechanism that returned the bridge to its normal position, the operator happened to look up toward the west and saw the oncoming NHRR train speeding down the tracks toward the river. At the speed the train was traveling, the operator realized it had no chance whatsoever of stopping before reaching the end of the bridge section.

The engineer and crew of the NHRR train apparently did not see the raised signal signifying the opening of the bridge. When it became apparent to them that the bridge was open, they jumped from the train.

Seconds later, the train, actually gaining speed, left the track and fell in a long, arcing flight into the Norwalk River. The engine, coal car, two mail cars, two passenger cars, and a freight car littered the river and formed an impassable barrier to boat traffic that would remain for almost two weeks.

Witnesses watched as freight, mail, luggage, and dead passengers spilled into the river from the broken and shattered railroad cars, got caught up in the current, and slowly floated out to sea. In all, forty-six people were killed, among them Birke.

For days, railroad crews, city workers, and citizen volunteers worked to remove the wreckage from the river and salvage anything of value. Some of the freight was recovered, but most of it was lost, having floated out into the estuary or sunk into the soft sands of the bottom of the channel.

The two jewelry-filled chests belonging to the late Thaddeus Birke were never recovered, and experts believe they still lie somewhere under several feet of river silt at the bottom of the Norwalk Channel.

The *Neptune's* Inland Cache

Though piracy was common up and down the east coast of North America for well over two hundred years, it was rare that the ocean-going freebooters were ever found more than just a few miles inland. An exception to this involves noted British brigand David Marteen, who, according to researchers, cached approximately $20 million worth of gold coins in Hartford County, less than five miles from the Massachusetts border.

Captain David Marteen, a pirate who gained notoriety for his daring raids on Atlantic merchantmen and shoreline communities during the 1650s, pulled off one of the greatest robberies in the history of piracy. In 1655, his ship attacked and captured the Spanish galleon *Neptune*. A large merchant ship, the *Neptune* had just departed a small island in the West Indies where it had stopped to take on fresh water. It carried $20 million worth of gold coins packed in several wooden trunks.

During the raid, Marteen's crew killed everyone aboard the *Neptune* and transferred the gold to the hold of the pirate ship. The *Neptune* was then scuttled, and Marteen set sail for the island of Tortuga just off the north coast of Venezuela. Tortuga had long served as a favorite retreat for Marteen, and here he and his sailors relaxed for weeks at a time in the relative safety of this easily defensible island.

During the journey to Tortuga, another pirate vessel appeared on the northern horizon and approached Marteen's ship. When the vessel came within range, the newcomer fired several cannon shots at Marteen's ship, all of which missed. Not wishing to do battle with the ship and risk the loss of the gold, Marteen ordered full sail ahead to Tortuga, and eventually the pirate ship outdistanced the pursuer.

Once docked at Tortuga, Marteen stationed guards along several miles of shoreline to keep a constant watch for the strange ship. Convinced that whoever commanded the ship knew about his treasure in gold, the pirate captain had the trunks offloaded and buried in a secret location just beyond the beach. Two weeks later, Marteen, certain the attacking ship had departed the area, organized his pirate crew and set sail once again to pillage ships and villages along the Atlantic Coast. The $20 million in gold was left behind, its location known only to the pirate captain.

For eight months, Marteen plundered trading vessels and conducted raids on defenseless coastal towns, but the ventures were seldom profitable. During the entire time, the captain fretted about his huge cache of gold coins on the island of Tortuga, fearful that someone would discover it, dig it up, and carry it away. Unable to control his fears and paranoia, Marteen decided to return to the island stronghold, unearth his treasure, and rebury it in a place where he was certain no one could ever find it.

For nearly a year, Marteen carried the gold-filled chests in the hold of his ship, hoping to find a satisfactory hiding place. Sometime in 1657 while planning a series of raids on coastal settlements, Marteen and his pirates were relaxing in the quiet waters of Long Island Sound along the coast of Connecticut. As Marteen explored the sound, he chanced upon the estuary of the Connecticut River. Impressed with the depth and width of the river, he decided to sail upstream to explore the area and perhaps locate a suitable site where he might cache his fortune.

The winds were favorable, and several days later Marteen's ship had sailed inland up the river, finally landing at a point just east of the present-day town of Windsor. Today, Windsor boasts a population of approximately eighteen thousand people, but during the mid-seventeenth century it consisted only of a few scattered farms, a church, and a tavern.

After dropping anchor near the west bank of the Connecticut River, Marteen spent several days searching in the nearby woods for a suitable place to bury his treasure.

During the time the pirates remained encamped here, groups of townspeople from nearby Windsor gathered atop low hills overlooking the river and observed the newcomers. The citizens never ventured from the safety of their observation posts, but Marteen noted the watchers appeared to be well armed and seemed hostile at the pirates' presence.

One day as he was searching in the woods far from the scrutiny of the Windsor citizens, Marteen found an ideal place to bury his treasure. In the dark of night, the pirate captain, along with several crewmen, carried the heavy chests from the ship to the hiding place and buried them three feet deep. After covering the cache with forest debris so it would look like any other part of the woods, Marteen told his men to prepare to leave the area. The next morning, the pirates boarded the ship, followed the river back to Long Island Sound, and sailed off once again in search of more booty, more adventure.

Relieved at the departure of the pirates, the Windsor residents, completely unaware of the treasure's existence, returned to their normal activities.

After two more years at sea, Marteen grew fearful once again that someone would find his treasure and steal it from him. He decided to return to the Connecticut River and check on it. Within two days after the pirate ship dropped anchor in the same location as before, the residents of Windsor were once again seen watching the pirates from their vantage points.

After several days, a group of watchers approached the pirate camp and sought an audience with the leader. During the subsequent discussion, the villagers told Marteen that they were uncomfortable with the presence of the pirates, that the newcomers were not welcome, and that they must leave immediately. Marteen's first inclination was to engage the farmers in a fight, but seeing that he and his crew were clearly outnumbered, he decided against it. Instead, Marteen assured the villagers that he and his men meant them no harm. The pirate captain requested permission to remain in camp for another two weeks. After that, he said, he and his crew would leave, never to return. The villagers agreed to this proposition and went back to their homes.

Instead of loading the gold onto the ship and returning to sea, Marteen decided to search for a more suitable hiding place even farther inland. With several stout crewmen transporting the heavy gold chests, Marteen led them northwestward from the river. After circling Windsor, the odd caravan continued deep into the Connecticut woods and beyond.

Eventually, the pirates arrived at the river's bank, which, according to their description, could be none other than the east fork of Salmon Brook. At this point, the pirates were less than a mile from where the stream confluences with the west fork. Here, the gold was buried, and its location marked with cryptic signs on nearby exposed stones.

Marteen returned once again to the high seas and piracy, but never again to Connecticut. He, along with his entire crew, were killed at sea a year later during a raid on a British merchantman.

During the 1920s, Richard Nelson, a Hartford County resident, learned about the buried Marteen treasure when he examined some old documents in a Boston library. Subsequent research, along with a number of interviews, led Nelson to believe the great pirate treasure was buried not far from the town of East Granby and on the banks of the east fork of Salmon Brook. For months, Nelson searched throughout the area for some indication of a cache.

One day while exploring along the east bank of Salmon Brook, Nelson discovered a large, exposed rock that bore a number of strange symbols and odd lettering. During subsequent searches over the next few months, he found several other stones, large and small, bearing similar markings. Nelson was certain the inscriptions on the stones bore information pertaining to Marteen's buried gold cache, but he was never able to interpret any of the clues.

About three years later, Nelson invited a friend and neighbor, Anthony Ruches, to help him try and locate Marteen's buried treasure. Together, the two men hiked up and down the east bank of Salmon Brook for two miles on several occasions in search of a logical burying place. When they weren't looking for the treasure, the two men spent their time attempting to decipher the markings on the stones.

During the course of several expeditions to the Salmon Brook area, Nelson and Ruches eventually collected all of the inscription-bearing rocks and carried them back to Ruches's home in East Granby where they could be studied at leisure.

Years passed, and Nelson, now elderly, grew too old to continue the search. When Nelson died around 1970, Ruches shipped the stones to an archeologist at a university in New York. Several months later, Ruches received a report that confirmed what he and Nelson believed all along—the symbols indicated there was indeed buried treasure consisting of gold coins somewhere along the banks of the east fork of Salmon Brook. The markings also provided an estimate of the cache's value as well as who buried it. The inscriptions were made, according to the archeologist, "by a man named Robert Caldwell or Robert Campbell." Subsequent research by Ruches revealed that a pirate named Robert Caldwell had served with David Marteen during his voyages up the Connecticut River.

The most disturbing news from the man who studied the markings, according to Ruches, was that the information on the rocks was only useful if they were being interpreted while the rocks were located in their *original* positions. It had been years since the rocks were removed, and Ruches had no recollection of their original positions or locations.

Ruches returned to the Salmon Brook region a number of times, always hopeful of finding some new sign of the Marteen cache, but it was not to be. Increasingly crippled with arthritis, Ruches eventually abandoned his search for the treasure.

According to a number of people who have researched this treasure, Marteen's $20 million worth of gold coins, buried somewhere along the east bank of the east fork of Salmon Brook more than three hundred years ago, is still there. It is estimated this cache would be worth well over $250 million if found today.

The Lost Washington Dollars

Pirate David Marteen's lost cache of gold coins is not the only buried treasure associated with the east fork of Connecticut's Salmon Brook. During the Revolutionary War, several wooden chests filled with specially minted gold coins were stolen from the Continental Army near East Granby and hastily buried near the stream. Aside from only a few, the coins, worth $2.5 million in 1779, have never been recovered.

During the 1770s, Lemuel Bates owned a tavern a short distance north of East Granby. The tavern, which served meals and spirits and rented rooms, was located along a route often used by travelers going from Boston to Philadelphia and back. In 1778, Bates was promoted to the rank of captain in the Continental Army, and Revolutionists often used the establishment as a meeting place.

Late one evening in 1779, a caravan consisting of thirteen wagons, each pulled by a team of four horses, pulled up to Bates's place of business. The wagon train had departed Boston several days earlier and was bound for Philadelphia, a long journey to the west. In need of rest and food, the caravan's leader climbed down from the front wagon and entered the tavern to make arrangements for lodging and meals.

While the newcomer spoke with Bates, several townsfolk gathered around the parked wagons and examined them. It was not often that a wagon train of this size passed through East Granby, and the citizens were curious. As the people approached the wagons, a number of men dressed in Continental Army uniforms, brandished weapons and warned them away.

Trunks and chests, many containing supplies and ammunition, were piled in the wagons. Several chests, however, were filled with gold coins, specially minted dollars bearing the likeness of George Washington. These coins, referred to as "Washington Dollars," had been minted in France and represented a loan from the French government for the struggling Continental Congress. Though the actual value of this shipment of gold coins has been debated throughout history, most experts who have studied this event have concluded it was approximately $2.5 million.

After negotiations for meals and lodging were completed, the men pulled the wagons around to the rear of the tavern and arranged them in a circle. Several armed guards were posted to keep watch over the vehicles and their contents.

During the night, word of the wagon train and its contents spread throughout the region, and, in a short time, a group of British sympathizers—the Tories—gathered in secret at a local official's home and made plans to seize the gold.

Later that same night, the Tories crept toward the guarded wagon train and remained in hiding for about two hours. Then, at a signal, they suddenly attacked the guards, killing them all. After quickly hitching the horses up to the wagons, the Tories drove them away toward the west into the night.

When the sleeping soldiers awoke at dawn to find their com-rades dead and the wagons gone, they immediately initiated a search. About two hours later, the wagons and teams were found in a farmer's pasture a short distance from the Bates Tavern. From the condition of the horses, it was apparent that they had been driven a long distance and returned. A quick examination of the wagons revealed that every chest containing the Washington Dollars was missing.

The soldiers attempted to locate the stolen gold. For several days, area houses and farms were searched, but the money was never found.

In the 1880s, Richard H. Phelps, a Hartford County resident, wrote a book about the region's history, and briefly described the theft of the Washington Dollars at Bates Tavern on that night in 1779.

In another part of his book, Phelps related the story of one Henry Wooster. Wooster, an East Granby resident who was often in trouble with the law, was also a Tory. Several months following the theft of the Washington Dollars, Wooster was convicted of stealing a neighbor's cattle and had been sentenced to Old Newgate Prison, located just outside of East Granby. After serving about six months, Wooster escaped from the prison, made his way to the coast, and eventually fled to England and safety.

Months later, Wooster's mother, still living in East Granby, received a letter from her son in which he confessed to his part in stealing the chests filled with Washington Dollars from the Continental Army.

According to Wooster's letter, the entire wagon train had been driven from Bates Tavern by the group of Tories to the banks of the east fork of Salmon Brook. Here, the coins were buried with the understanding that they would be excavated later and used to aid the British in the war effort.

Just as the hiding place was being filled in with dirt, dawn broke over the woods. Moments later, the Tories climbed onto the wagons and returned to East Granby. After abandoning the wagons in a local farmer's field, Wooster said the men returned to their homes, sworn to secrecy.

Several weeks later, the Tories agreed to meet at a remote location in the woods to decide the fate of the coins. As they were discussing the matter, they were attacked by Indians and everyone but Wooster was killed. Wooster intended to return to the cache and retrieve the gold, but he was caught stealing a neighbor's cow and sent to prison. Wooster never returned from England, and in his letter, he was never able to provide accurate directions relative to the location of the buried Washington Dollars.

Though a few East Granby residents searched for the buried treasure during the months after it was stolen, the tale of this Tory cache was largely forgotten until 1944.

Several days following a period of heavy rains and flooding throughout Hartford County, a man was hiking along the bank of the east fork of Salmon Brook when a glint in the stream caught his eye. Wading into the waters, he retrieved the object of his attention—a Washington Dollar!

After the coin's finder told his story in East Granby, a number of citizens arrived at the stream to search for the Tory treasure they believed to be still located nearby. Some contended that the flooded stream eroded into a bank, exposing the buried, and likely rotted, chests of gold. Though the searchers examined the area closely for several days, nothing more was found.

In 1958, two teenage boys who were playing near Salmon Brook found three strange coins. Several days later, one of the boys showed the coins to his father who, after consulting several references, identified them as Washington Dollars. The youth told his father that the coins were found on the bank of the east fork of Salmon Brook.

A few days later, the father and the two boys returned to the area, but the exact location where the coins were initially discovered could not be found.

149

In 1987, another Washington Dollar was discovered. A woman driving west on Highway 20 had a flat tire just as she reached the bridge that spanned the east fork of Salmon Brook. When she finished changing the flat, she walked down to the stream and washed her hands. While kneeling at the bank, she spotted a round, shiny object lying among the stream gravel about three feet away. After retrieving it, she discovered it was a coin, later identified as a Washington Dollar.

Many who have remained close to this tale believe that the wooden chests containing the Washington Dollars have long since rotted away, freeing the encased coins. Subsequent bank erosion and stream undercutting has likely exposed the cache site, allowing some, or all, of the coins to spill into the stream bed. Since gold is relatively heavy and seldom travels far except in swiftly running streams, it is likely that the original site of the buried coins is not far from the spots of recent discoveries.

Nest of Gold Coins

There is nothing left of J. O. Maloney's original Litchfield County farm. In fact, many who have taken the trouble to research pertinent documents remain uncertain as to its exact location and extent. Litchfield died around 1890, leaving no heirs. What he did leave, however, was a fortune in gold and silver coins that the old man kept hidden in a secret location and that many have searched for but none have found.

Well over one hundred years ago, J. O. Maloney operated a small farm just outside the present-day town of Morris, located at the intersection of state roads 61 and 109 in Litchfield County. Maloney, who never married and had no living relatives when he died, was regarded by his neighbors as a very frugal and rather eccentric man who preferred solitude. He was seldom seen in town except on the rare occasions when he arrived to conduct business.

Maloney never employed any farmhands and, despite his estimated age of around seventy, he operated his farm completely by himself. It was not uncommon to see the old man working in his field from before dawn until long past sunset. As a result of the attention and care he devoted to his farm, Maloney prospered nicely. In fact, he grew wealthy.

Maloney's reputation as an industrious and successful farmer grew in the region. The income he derived from selling livestock and feed over the years was never deposited in a bank; the old man harbored a deep distrust for such institutions. After many years of successful business transactions, it was common knowledge that Maloney had amassed a sizeable fortune. Once, when a neighbor asked Maloney what he did with his money, the farmer replied that he hid it in a secret place where no one could ever find it.

When J. O. Maloney died around 1890, his funeral was brief and few people attended. The old farmer had not been in the ground for more than a week, however, when neighbors began wondering aloud where he could possibly have hidden his money. From time to time, the curious went to Maloney's farm, searched through his house, and dug holes in the ground looking for his reputed hoard, but they never found anything.

About a year following Maloney's death, two brothers from Litchfield were visiting relatives in Morris, and they decided to go squirrel hunting in the woods adjacent to Maloney's now ne-glected farm. During the hunt, one of the hunters spotted a squirrel perched on a tree limb about fourteen feet above the ground and shot at it. The animal, slightly wounded, immediately scurried into a hole in the tree where the limb joined the trunk.

The hunter, determined to retrieve his prize, climbed the tree and reached into the nest in search of the wounded animal.

Not finding the squirrel, the hunter withdrew a fistful of nest material and was surprised to discover it consisted of chewed and shredded currency! Several more withdrawals from the squirrel hole yielded more of the tiny remnants of paper money.

On returning to Morris, the hunters told the story of finding the fragmented currency. Excitedly, townspeople related the tale of farmer Maloney's hidden treasure. It was little wonder that it was never found in or near the house. Maloney had apparently concealed it in a squirrel's nest high in a tree and far from his dwelling. During the time it had been hidden, squirrels had discovered it and found the currency was suitable for nesting material.

The Morris citizens also told the squirrel hunters that, in addition to the currency, Maloney was known to possess a fortune in gold and silver coins and that the coins had likely been cached along with the currency.

Excited at the prospect of locating a fortune in coins in the squirrel hole, the hunters made preparations to return to the site. As they prepared to leave, however, they were troubled by the large number of townspeople who gathered to follow them. Not wishing company during their search for the treasure, the hunters decided instead to return home to Litchfield and return to search for Maloney's treasure another time.

On two subsequent occasions, the hunters traveled to Maloney's farm to look for the tree where the currency had been found, but both times they were seen arriving. Word quickly spread among Morris residents, who dropped whatever they were doing to follow the brothers into the woods. Each time, the hunters promptly discontinued their search and returned to Litchfield.

Several months passed, and once again the two hunters made arrangements to travel to Maloney's farm and try to retrieve the gold and silver coins they believed were hidden in the squirrel's nest. This time, they avoided the town of Morris by circling it a mile to the west and entering the woods without being spotted. After several hours of searching throughout the area, however, all of the trees looked much the same to them. Having neglected to mark the location of the tree containing the money-filled nest, the two hunters realized that locating it now would be virtually impossible.

During the next three years, the two hunters returned to the Maloney farm from time to time to try to locate the tree but were never successful.

In 1937, two young boys playing in the woods located just outside Morris found a gold coin on the ground. The coin had an 1886 mint date, and many who inspected it believed that it was likely part of Maloney's hoard. The discovery revived the tale of the old farmer's hidden treasure, and the woods were once again filled with searchers.

Today, an occasional visitor to the Litchfield County seat will request property records from the 1880s. From the descriptions, the approximate location of J. O. Maloney's farm is determined, and shortly thereafter the newcomer will be seen searching through the woods.

To date, no discovery of Maloney's coin cache has ever been announced, and it is presumed to still lie hidden in the hollow of an old tree.

During the time that has passed since Maloney's death, it is quite possible that the tree the farmer used as a cache has died, rotted, and fallen over. As the tree succumbs to gradual decomposition, Maloney's coins will likely be released from their hiding place and spill onto the forest floor.

Here they may lie forever, or perhaps some fortunate hiker will unexpectedly stumble upon them during an outing.

An Incredible Find on Fairfield Beach

In 1822, a pirate ship of unknown origin, but believed to be Spanish, anchored in Long Island Sound just off Connecticut's Penfield Reef near the present-day town of Fairfield. After laying at anchor until just after nightfall, a ship lowered a longboat filled with pirates into the sound and they begain rowing to Fairfield Beach, the closest landing. After pulling the boat several feet onto the shore and out of the water, the pirates lifted out five large porcelain crocks and laid them on the sands. Each crock was only about fourteen inches tall and eight inches in diameter, but they were filled to the top with gold coins. It took several trips, but the heavy crocks were transported with great difficulty to a location in the nearby dunes several yards above the high tide level where a wide trench was being dug. The pirates buried the crocks approximately four feet deep. Before filling in the shallow excavation, one of the pirates killed another by bashing him in the head with a shovel. The dead man was subsequently thrown into the hole, landing face-up on the crocks. Pirates believed the fewer people who knew about the treasure the better. Killing one of their own to keep their loot a secret didn't bother the ruthless mariners. After refilling the trench, the pirates walked back to the longboat and rowed to their ship. The next morning, the pirate vessel had vanished.

For sixty-two years, this buried treasure lay undisturbed until it was accidentally discovered by an elderly couple during a walk on the beach. A portion of the cache was retrieved, but the couple missed the largest part of it. It is presumed that it still lies buried somewhere on Fairfield Beach.

Around 1868, George and Mabel Hawley moved to the peninsula that terminates at Pine Creek Point in southwestern Connecticut, a short distance from the town of Fairfield. They built a simple, rustic cabin to live out their golden years. Hawley, sixty-one years old had recently retired as a freighter, and he and his wife looked forward to living a quiet life of relative leisure near Long Island Sound. Fairfield Beach wasn't far from the Hawleys's residence, and it was here they spent many pleasant hours hiking in the dunes and collecting interesting shells, pieces of driftwood, and occasional artifacts washed ashore from ships that sank in the sound many years earlier.

One day in 1884, while walking alone on a section of the beach near Penfield Reef, George Hawley found a small, black, circular object lying in the sand. Curious, he put it in his pocket and made a mental note to examine it closer when he returned home. Several days later, Hawley remembered the object, retrieved it, and took it into the kitchen to scrub the dark residue from the surface. When it had finally been cleaned, Hawley was surprised and delighted to discover it was a gold coin—an American $10 piece minted in 1795.

Several days later, Hawley took the coin to a collector in Bridgeport who offered him an impressive sum of money for it. The retired freighter decided not to sell the coin until, as he confidently informed the collector, he could bring in a few more hundred of them. On the way home, Hawley grew more and more convinced that the coin was only one of many to find on the beach. Perhaps, he considered, a large pirate treasure was buried somewhere nearby, and it was just possible he could find it.

For nearly four years, Hawley, sometimes accompanied by his wife, returned to the portion of Fairfield Beach where he first found the coin and searched for hours, convinced he would find more and eventually discover the cache from which he believed it came.

In November 1888, a violent storm, struck. Ships were sunk, coastal communities were devastated, and the fishing industry was disrupted for several weeks. The high winds and waves were also responsible for an incredible amount of coastline modification, including the washing away of large portions of beaches along the Long Island Sound shores.

Several days following what has since been called the Great November Gale, George Hawley visited Fairfield Beach only to discover that the topography, along with the coastline, had changed dramatically because of the storm. Hawley feared that the effects from the gale had ultimately dashed his hopes of ever finding the lost pirate treasure he believed to be buried here.

Several months passed, and one day Mabel Hawley packed a lunch and suggested to George that they have a picnic on the beach. Looking out the window, Hawley noticed a stiff wind was blowing, and he tried to discourage the idea of an outing. Mabel, however, was not to be deterred.

Two hours later, carrying sack lunches, the Hawleys, with their hats pulled down and coats buttoned up against the strong wind and stinging sand, walked along the beach. Presently, they found a suitable log and, backs to the wind, leaned against it, ate their sandwiches, and drank coffee. By the time they finished, the wind lessened, and the two decided to continue on their afternoon walk.

As George and Mabel hiked along the beach, they gradually separated and proceeded along about forty yards apart. Hawley noticed that the strong and consistent winds had removed a great deal of the surface sand, exposing long-buried shells and drift-wood. Here and there, he came across broken artifacts, likely objects washed up from some long-forgotten shipwreck.

As George was engrossed in picking items out of the sand, he was suddenly startled by a piercing scream from his wife. Hurrying toward the sound, he found her in a dead faint. After failing to revive her immediately, he lifted her and, with great difficulty, carried her back to the house.

When Mabel Hawley finally came around, she told her husband an incredible story. As she was hiking along in the dunes, she, like George, became fascinated with the large number of objects that had been exposed by the wind-driven, shifting sands. A shallow depression was near her route, and when she looked into it she saw, looking back up at her, a human skull. At that point, she fainted.

As Mabel Hawley slept the rest of the afternoon, George, searching through some books on the mantlepiece, found a brief reference to the curious practice of some pirates who occasionally killed one of their own and placed the body atop a cache of buried treasure. Believing there might be a connection between this and Mabel's recent experience, he determined to return to the beach the next morning. Dawn of the following day, however, brought heavy rains that lasted for a week.

Finally, the sky cleared and George Hawley, carrying a shovel and a canteen filled with water, returned to the beach. For several hours he traced and retraced the approximate route that he and his wife followed during their earlier walk. Eventually, he came across a barely discernible and quite shallow depression in the sand and paused to investigate.

The recent rains had mixed with the sands, and the depression had smoothed out and was almost filled to the level of the beach surface. Convinced, however, that this was the location where his wife fainted, Hawley poked around in the sand with the tip of the spade. Presently, he struck something hard.

Carefully digging away a few inches of sand, he uncovered the top of a human skull. Dropping to his hands and knees, he carefully removed the rest of the sand from around the skull and lifted the object out of the hole. After setting it nearby, he probed the small crater further and encountered several rib bones, a leg bone, and eventually an entire human skeleton. The effort tired the old man, and he often paused often to rest.

By now, the sun was setting and the beach was growing dark. Hawley replaced the skull and bones in the hole, refilled it, made note of nearby landmarks, and left for home. As he slowly walked along, he was already making plans to return on the morrow to excavate even more sand and bones in the hope of finding a pirate cache.

Hawley was awake and making preparations for another trip to the beach three hours before dawn. After packing a lunch, he grabbed his shovel and left the house while sunrise was still thirty minutes away.

This time, Hawley walked directly to the spot he excavated the previous day and, after a short rest, began shoveling the sand out of the hole. Within a few minutes, the old man uncovered the skeleton and once again removed it from the pit. Just below the skeleton, however, the substrate was considerably denser and digging became increasingly difficult. More than the previous day, Hawley, now in his late seventies, found it necessary to stop and rest more often from his efforts.

After digging the hole four feet deep, Hawley began having a problem with sand spilling back into it. As a result, he spent more time and effort widening the excavation. Presently, the tired man was once again forced to quit because of approaching dusk.

Without refilling the hole this time, Hawley returned home planning to arrive early again the next morning to resume his quest.

By noon on the following day, Hawley had managed to excavate the hole to six feet deep. Suddenly, his spade struck a solid object and, moments later, he was on his knees in the hole, digging with his hands and pulling sand away from what appeared to be a large porcelain crock. The jar stood just over twelve inches tall and had a diameter about the size of a large man's thigh. The crock's mouth appeared to be sealed with a type of mortar that was resistant to repeated taps from Hawley's shovel.

Hawley made several attempts to lift the crock out of the hole, but found it so heavy he was unable to budge it. Finally, he hammered away at it with his shovel until it finally broke. Suddenly, hundreds of gold coins spilled from the shattered container, completely covering Hawley's shoes as he stood in awe of his discovery. Picking up one of the coins, he saw that it was an American $10 gold piece with a 1795 mint date, just like the one he found four years earlier. While digging through the pile of coins, he also found British sovereigns and Spanish doubloons.

Once again it grew late in the day and Hawley had to return home. He stuffed his pockets with as many of the coins as they could hold and, with great difficulty, crawled out of the hole. He was so exhausted, he threw just enough sand into the excavation to cover the treasure, and, carrying his shovel, walked away.

Because he had to stop several times to rest, Hawley did not reach his house until very late. When he finally arrived, Mabel was waiting for him, frantic with worry. After kissing her in greeting, he informed her they were very rich, and he proceeded to unload the gold coins from his pockets.

The next day, Hawley and Mabel carried several burlap sacks back to the excavation. They worked the entire day picking the coins from the bottom of the pit and placing them in the containers. When they finally decided they had retrieved every one of them, they placed the skeleton back into the hole and refilled it for the last time.

A week later, Hawley transported an estimated one hundred pounds of gold into Bridgeport, converted it to cash, and he and Mabel lived the rest of their lives having fulfilled their dreams of becoming wealthy.

George and Mabel Hawley passed away during the final decade of the nineteenth century, but the story of their fabulous discovery lived on in the Fairfield and Bridgeport communities.

In 1931, a nautical researcher came across a strange and unexpected discovery in a Boston library while examining some shipping industry documents.

Among the books and records he was studying, the researcher encountered a old, ragged journal inside of which was a folded, brittle parchment map. Though the map came apart in several pieces when it was opened up, the researcher clearly recognized a sketch of the southern coastline of Connecticut. Perusing the journal, he thrilled as he read the account of a buried treasure by pirates in 1822. According to the description, five porcelain crocks were cached, each filled with booty taken from raids on American, British, and Spanish ships in the Atlantic Ocean. Given the relatively detailed map and the rather precise directions, the researcher decided to make a trip to Fairfield and try his luck at finding the treasure.

Shortly after arriving at the small Connecticut town, the researcher learned the story of George Hawley's amazing discovery years earlier. At first, he was disappointed that someone had beaten him to the treasure, but a short time later he was delighted and relieved to discover that Hawley only found one crock. The journal detailed the burial of five of them!

The researcher traveled to the beach only to discover that the contours of the present coastline bore absolutely no resemblance to those sketched on the map. Local residents explained how dramatically the beach is altered after every severe storm strikes the area. Given the present configuration of the coastline, the directions in the journal, as well as the map, were rendered quite useless, and the researcher quickly abandoned his quest.

Today, lying somewhere on the portion of Fairfield Beach not far from the shoreline that looks out over Penfield Reef, lies buried four porcelain crocks, each brimming with gold coins.

Old Leatherman's Treasure

Jules Bourglay, the second son of a prominent French business-man, grew up in a wealthy family, received a fine education, and, on reaching adulthood, was given a choice of managing several different family businesses. The young man decided to take charge of the Bourglay's extensive leather business and plunged into the task with youthful vigor and enthusiasm.

Bourglay, an extremely competent manager, often worked day and night, sometimes going forty-eight hours without sleep. He was so dedicated to the enterprise that, in addition to managing the company, he occasionally donned work clothes and spent hours in the factory at the processing vats with the workers tanning and cutting the hides.

After four very successful and profitable years, the market for leather garments and gloves in Europe weakened dramatically and a short time afterward Bourglay was forced to lay off employees and close the company's doors.

The impact of the failure of the business to which Bourglay had dedicated himself so entirely left him insane, according to his family, and they were unsuccessful in trying to get him interested in other enterprises. Finally, after packing a few belongings and his life savings of approximately $50,000 in gold coins, Bourglay, only twenty-five years old, left France forever and traveled to America.

After arriving at the port of New York, Bourglay, dressed in leather, purchased a wooden wheelbarrow. In the single-wheeled pushcart, he loaded some supplies and several leather sacks that contained his gold coins. After remaining in New York for about two months, Bourglay, pushing his wheelbarrow, started walking northeastward with no particular destination in mind.

Along the way, Bourglay occasionally stopped in small settlements to replenish supplies. By now he had grown a thick beard and his hair, having gone uncut for weeks, was quite long. His leather clothes bore the wear and grime of a long journey.

As residents of the tiny communities crowded around Bourglay for news, they soon realized the newcomer was deranged. Babbling in French, Bourglay attempted to relate various experiences he had encountered during his travels, but very few people could understand him. Invariably during these visits, Bourglay would open the leather sacks and show onlookers his fortune in gold. Stunned that a crazy, dirty man would travel alone carrying so much money in a wheelbarrow, the citizens merely stared in awe. It was remarkable that Bourglay was never robbed.

Eventually, Bourglay's wanderings took him to the small western Connecticut community of Harwinton, about five miles southeast of Torrington. As before, Bourglay showed anyone who approached him his gold, excitedly pointing to the shiny coins and explaining in his native tongue that they represented the fortune he earned in the leather business. Though Harwinton residents could not understand the Frenchman, they nevertheless welcomed him and invited him to stay. After sleeping near the edge of town for several days, Bourglay moved deeper into the woods and constructed a crude lean-to from fallen tree limbs and pine boughs.

In time, Bourglay found work in Harwinton as a carpenter and handyman. The residents accepted the mad, eccentric Frenchman and soon treated him as one of their own.

Bourglay always arrived at his job pushing the wheelbarrow ahead of him. He parked it nearby, and from time to time took a break from his task, went to the wheelbarrow, and looked at his coins. The Frenchman always invited passersby to examine the gold.

Bourglay remained in Harwinton for four years and was never seen without his wheelbarrow. One day, without any explanation whatsoever, the Frenchman was gone and never returned.

About two years later, Bourglay, pushing his wheelbarrow, showed up in New Haven, the busy Connecticut coastal city on Long Island Sound. Here, the residents were not as tolerant or accepting as those the Frenchman was used to. Though completely harmless and non-threatening, Bourglay was stoned and run out of town on the very afternoon he arrived.

Two days later, he walked into East Haven, located just across the bay from New Haven, and received a completely different reception. East Haven citizens readily accepted the Frenchman. When he expressed an interest in work, he was immediately hired by a local shopkeeper to stock shelves and sweep floors. Bourglay, still dressed in leather garments, was affectionately called Old Leatherman.

At the first opportunity, Bourglay showed his new friends the contents of his wheelbarrow. Amazed that the curious newcomer could travel around the country as he did without being attacked or robbed of his fortune, the East Haven citizens simply accepted his eccentricities and even became somewhat protective of their new resident.

Just to the northeast of New Haven lies Lake Saltonstall, and not far from the lake, Bourglay resided in what he described, using sign language, as a small cave. Each morning after rising, Bourglay loaded the leather sacks filled with gold coins into his wheelbarrow that he pushed into town on his way to work. As was his practice, Bourglay kept the wheelbarrow nearby as he went about his duties. In the evening when he was finished, he pushed it back to his cave.

Bourglay tried to describe his habitation to a few East Haven residents, but they never understood where it was actually located. During the time Bourglay lived in East Haven, some of the residents tried to visit him at his cave near the lake, but they were never able to find it. Because Bourglay could not speak English, he couldn't provide precise directions.

For approximately twenty years, Jules Bourglay lived contentedly in East Haven. He was a dependable employee, always arrived at his job early, and remained until his duties were completed. By now, he was well known by most East Haven residents who waved greetings to him each morning as he walked into town pushing his wheelbarrow. Virtually everyone in town had seen Bourglay's gold coins more than once, and the Frenchman never tired of showing them.

One morning, Bourglay did not show up for work. Worried that his employee might have met with an accident, the shopkeeper sent his youngest son to follow the trail that led to the lake and find Old Leatherman. On arriving near the southwestern end of Lake Saltonstall near the point where Farm River spills out on its way to Long Island Sound, the boy spotted Bourglay lying face down near the shoreline. The Frenchman was dead, apparently from a heart attack.

Later that same morning, the shopkeeper, along with two other East Haven residents, drove a wagon to the lake to retrieve Bourglay's body. The following day, the Frenchman was buried in the town cemetery, and almost the entire population of East Haven attended the funeral.

During the ensuing weeks, many East Haven citizens wondered about Bourglay's fortune in gold coins. When the body was found, neither the wheelbarrow nor the coins were anywhere about. On several different occasions, search parties went to Lake Saltonstall to try to find the cave where the reclusive Frenchman lived, but were unsuccessful.

For years, people searched for Bourglay's treasure, but no sign of his gold, his wheelbarrow, or even the cave was ever found. Initially, the searchers concentrated on Beacon Hill, a three-quarter mile long ridge extending southward from the lake. A section of Beacon Hill's northwestern slope extends to the Farm River where Bourglay's body was found.

In later years, treasure hunters believed that a small hill on the other side of Farm River was a more likely location for the Frenchman's cave, but still nothing was found.

Around the beginning of the twentieth century, a discovery was made that suggested Bourglay did not reside in a cave at all, but rather a dugout. An East Haven fisherman was trying his luck along the southern shore of Lake Saltonstall one afternoon when he spotted a wooden plank protruding out of a portion of nearby hillside. After trying to pull the piece of wood out of the ground, the fisherman discovered it was attached to something buried deeper in the low-angled slope.

After digging away some of the surface soil, the fisherman eventually uncovered a single wheel and several pieces of rotten planks nailed together. The wheel, about eighteen inches in diameter, was fitted with an iron rim. The fisherman determined that the wheel and planks were once part of a wheelbarrow. Keeping only the wheel as a curiosity, the fisherman returned home and set it against one wall of his house.

About twelve years later, the fisherman with a neighbor's help was cleaning up around his house and yard when he encountered the old and long-forgotten wheel. When the neighbor inquired about the curious object, the fisherman related its discovery.

Almost immediately, the neighbor grew excited and told the fisherman the tale of Old Leatherman's lost wheelbarrow full of gold coins.

Together, the two men returned to the southern shore of Lake Saltonstall in an attempt to relocate the place where the wheel had been dug from the ground, but each part of the low slope looked like the other.

As the news of the wheelbarrow's discovery spread around the area, dozens of people familiar with the story of the Frenchman's lost gold arrived at Lake Saltonstall to search for the treasure, but nothing was ever found.

Today, researchers and professional treasure hunters alike agree that Jules Bourglay likely lived in a dugout, not a cave, and that following his death, natural circumstances simply caused the dugout to cave in, covering the wheelbarrow and the leather sacks filled with gold coins.

Since the coins were not likely to be very deep in the ground, their discovery and retrieval would normally be a simple matter of scanning the slope with sophisticated metal detectors.

Unfortunately, the construction of the Boston Post Road directly across the slope has either covered the coins or significantly modified the area such that it may impossible to ever locate the treasure.

If found, Old Leatherman's gold coins would be worth well over $1 million at today's values.

RHODE ISLAND

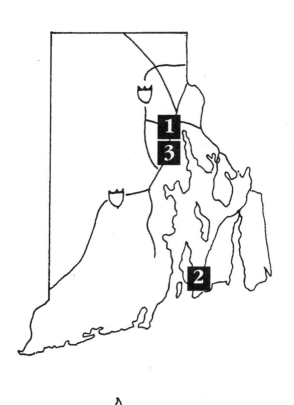

The Mystery of the Lost Silver Bell

One of the most enduring and perplexing mysteries in Rhode Island is connected to the so-called lost silver church bell that once hung in a Providence church tower. The bell, finely crafted by a seventeenth century Dutch silversmith, was fashioned from almost pure silver and weighed five hundred pounds. During the next two hundred and twenty-eight years, this spectacular creation disappeared three times, and after the third time the bell vanished, in 1891, it was not seen again. Many believe it is hidden somewhere within the Providence city limits.

The Providence Bell, as it has come to be called, was made by noted Dutch silversmith Peter Seest in Amsterdam in 1663. The silver used by Seest reputedly came from rich mines in Mexico via Spain and was refined several times in order to achieve the purity that he believed necessary for the ultimate tone of this incredible bell. Originally intended for placement in an Amsterdam church tower, the bell mysteriously disappeared. One year later it showed up in the United States. To this day, no one knows how it arrived in this country or who was responsible.

On January 1, 1665, the silver bell was hung in the tower of a Providence church where it rang in the new year. Providence residents enjoyed the ringing celebration of each new year for the next ninety-one years. The silver bell was also rung to announce the beginning of Sunday services, for marriages, and other celebrations.

The silver bell became a source of pride for Providence residents, but, for unexplained reasons, it was removed from the tower in 1756 and shipped to England where it was installed in a convent. In England, the bell was rung at dawn each day to summon the nuns to the worship services.

Sometime later—history does not record the exact date—pirates stormed the convent and the neighboring community. In addition to looting stores and warehouses, the brigands stole valuables from residents and travelers. Before the raid was over, the pirates took the silver bell from the convent and carried it aboard ship.

What became of the bell during the next several decades is unknown, but, curiously, it showed up again in the most mysterious of circumstances during the War of 1812. An American vessel patrolling a portion of the Atlantic Ocean near Massachusetts engaged a British warship in battle. Subsequently, the British boat was captured and, during a search of the hold, the silver bell was found wrapped in a canvas sail and lying among crates of supplies and ammunition. An explanation of why the bell was on the British ship was never given.

After several months, the bell was eventually returned to Providence where it was hung once again in the same church tower where it previously resided.

Eventually, the old and now crumbling Providence church needed maintenance and repair. Prior to rebuilding the church tower, however, the silver bell had to be removed. Once that formidable task was accomplished, the heavy object was stored in the chambers of an assistant priest.

A strange man, known only by the name Grayson, was employed by the church during this time. Grayson was an eldritch-like, dwarfish groundskeeper who had been born with one leg about eight inches shorter than the other and a pronounced hump on his back. This congenital disfigurement caused Grayson to hobble clumsily about his duties and made him an object of scorn and ridicule among Providence residents, particularly children, who taunted and made fun of the unfortunate man at every opportunity.

To add to Grayson's somewhat frightening appearance, he was nearly toothless and his ruddy-colored skin was host to a number of untreated pustules. The groundskeeper seldom bathed and never cut his hair, which hung in dirty, clumped tendrils to the middle of his back. Grayson had only one eye—his left. The right eye, according to town gossip, was burned out when he was much younger by pirates using a hot poker, leaving a dark cavity ringed by scar tissue. It was whispered that Grayson had once served aboard a pirate ship in his youth.

Despite Grayson's deformities, he was uncommonly strong and often called upon to lift and move heavy objects during the course of his workday, which he did with relative ease. In fact, Grayson almost single-handedly transported the silver bell to its resting place in the priest's quarters.

While stonemasons were busy with the repair and rebuilding of the church tower, the silver bell mysteriously disappeared.

Frantic, church officials conducted searches of the buildings and grounds, but were unable to find the precious bell. After several weeks, they stopped looking, and the cherished Providence Bell's whereabouts remained a mystery.

More time passed, and church officials and Providence townsfolk forgot about the lost silver bell.

Late one evening, approximately one year following the bell's disappearance, Grayson, still in the employ of the church, entered a dockside Providence tavern called The Dolphin and seated himself at a table with four sinister-looking men. The quartet, all rough and surly, were dressed like pirates and carried several sabers and knives tucked in their sashes. They had arrived the previous day on a ship anchored a considerable distance out in the harbor, far from the curious stares of dockside workers and authorities.

The newcomers were not known by any of the regular patrons of the tavern, and after Grayson's arrival, they spoke in hushed tones while they ordered several rounds of ale.

According to drinkers who were close enough to overhear the conversation, Grayson told the newcomers about the missing silver bell, claimed he knew where it was hidden, and offered to sell it to them for the equivalent of $100. Grayson and the men haggled for several minutes, and soon an argument broke out. One of the pirates seated at the table suddenly struck the groundskeeper across the face with the hilt of a long knife, opening a long and bloody wound on one cheek. Seconds later, Grayson, clearly upset, hobbled out of the tavern. It was the last time anyone saw him alive.

Shortly after dawn of the following day, two fishermen discovered Grayson's body lying on the shore where the Providence Harbor narrows. His throat had been cut.

Historians who have studied this aspect of Providence history have concluded that Grayson, believing he would be able to sell the silver bell to the pirates, stole it from the priest's room where it was being stored. Given Grayson's great strength, it falls within the realm of possibility that he, alone, could have dragged, rolled, or somehow carted the bell to another location and hidden it.

When the opportunity presented itself, Grayson attempted to bargain with men he believed would meet his price for the precious bell. They didn't, and in the ensuing disagreement, Grayson, apparently the only person who knew the secret location of the bell, was killed.

It is reasonable to think that Grayson, regardless of his strength, did not transport the heavy bell very far. It is further assumed that the object was hidden, probably buried, somewhere not far from the old church.

Following a careful study of Providence history, it is also considered likely that the bell, which carries with it a remarkable history, is still hidden somewhere in old downtown Providence. If found today, the Providence bell would be considered a priceless historical artifact.

Bloody Tew's Lost Gold

During the late 1600s and early 1700s, Joseph Thomas Tew as he was called, conducted his piratical activities with a certain colorful flair. He was always seen garbed in a heavy, long-tailed woolen coat and long flowing cape, even in summer. Wide leather belts carrying knives, pistols, and swords crisscrossed his coated torso. Tew sported a well-trimmed goatee and wore a long red silk scarf around his neck.

An expert swordsman, Bloody Tew often lined up as many as ten captives on his ship's deck and, one by one, engaged them in a sword fight. Reputedly, Tew smiled and laughed throughout the competition as he dazzled observers and opponents alike with his keen fighting skills. After dispatching the last of his victims, Tew would hang the bodies upside down from the ship's railings as trophies.

After seven years of successful raiding and pillaging of ships and settlements in the Caribbean and along the Atlantic Coast, Bloody Tew amassed an incredible fortune in booty. Though never authenticated, stories abounded that Tew kept an extra ship in his fleet for the sole purpose of transporting his staggering wealth of gold and silver coins and ingots.

The years of piracy were good to Joseph Tew, but he eventually fell upon hard times. Time and again, the British, French, and Americans attacked Tew's fleet in increasing numbers, and the pirate eventually suffered one defeat after another. During a battle off the coast of Virginia, Tew's treasure ship was sunk deep in the continental shelf waters. An uncountable fortune that has never been found went down with the ship.

Tiring of the constant pursuit and harassment, Bloody Tew finally decided to give up pirating and settled onto a plot of land that he purchased just outside Newport. Even though he lost his fabulous treasure, Tew managed to retire with approximately $200,000 in gold coins that he cached at a secret location somewhere on his property.

Changing his name to Carter, Bloody Tew lived in Newport for four years. On occasion, he would have Tolliver, his servant, drive him to town in the carriage. While Tolliver purchased provisions, Tew enjoyed quaffing ales and flirting with maidens at the local taverns. Though it was rumored that Carter was actually a feared pirate, he quietly went about his business, and, though he continued to wear his coat, cape, and red sash, maintained a low profile and lived a peaceful life. There were times, however, when Tew grew bored with city life and longed for the adventure of piracy. He found himself missing the sea, the thrill of combat, and the stealing of treasure. Early one morning when three of his former crewmen arrived at his door and begged him to return to the sea and lead them on a raiding venture, Tew could not resist. Informing Tolliver he would be away for several months, he packed a duffel containing his long coat, cape, and sash, and left with his companions.

Weeks later, Bloody Tew led his charges against a British privateer off the Maine coast. During the battle, Tew's vessel caught fire. When flames reached the ship's magazine, the resulting explosion blew a huge hole in the bow and, within a few minutes, the ship sank. There were no survivors.

The following morning, a sailor on a British ship spotted a long red sash floating in the waters near where the pirate ship went down.

Within a few weeks, coastal residents learned about Bloody Tew's death. Shortly afterward, Newport citizens discovered that their neighbor Carter and the feared pirate Joseph Thomas Tew were one and the same.

One afternoon, about three months after Bloody Tew's ship sank, a young man arrived at Newport in a handsome new carriage. He identified himself as Richard Tew and drove directly to the residence of the late pirate. The servant, Tolliver, who was in the process of packing his few belongings before moving out, greeted Young Tew at the door. Richard Tew informed Tolliver that he was the son of the pirate Bloody Tew. Young Tew also told the servant of his intention to occupy the house for a time and asked Tolliver to remain.

After Tolliver unloaded young Tew's belongings from the carriage and deposited them in the house, he unhitched the horses and led them to the barn for grooming. While the servant was thus occupied, Richard Tew approached him and asked if he knew where his father had hidden his treasure. Tolliver stated that he never knew, only that on occasion the elder Tew would disappear in the woods behind the house for an hour at a time, always returning with a sack of gold coins.

Richard Tew searched the area behind the house for trails during the next few days but found none. Apparently Bloody Tew, always careful and wary, took a different route to his treasure cache each time he needed some funds, never leaving any sign of his passage.

Having no luck finding a path, Richard Tew enlisted Tolliver's aid, and together the two men searched for evidence of an excavation. None seemed to exist.

As young Tew and Tolliver explored the woods during their searches for Bloody Tew's cache, they often passed a large tree with an extremely thick trunk. About eight feet from the ground, a large hole in the tree was evident. When Tew asked Tolliver about it, the servant stated that he sometimes hunted squirrels that lived in the tree's hollow bole.

For three years, Richard Tew resided in his father's home. A week never passed that he did not venture into the woods behind the house searching for the secret cache of the pirate. Finally, convinced he would never locate the gold, Richard Tew sold the house, paid Tolliver a handsome severance, packed his effects into the carriage, and drove away. He was never seen again.

Rumors of Bloody Tew's buried treasure circulated up and down the Atlantic Coast for years, and men sometimes arrived to search the woods behind the house. Though dozens of holes were excavated throughout the property, no treasure was ever found. The location of the Tew treasure cache became a perplexing mystery, and after several years of fruitless searching, many people began to believe it never actually existed. Though a provocative legend, few people bothered to search for it any longer even though several versions of the tale had been recorded in regional folklore books.

In 1880, however, an event occurred that lent credence to the tale. During the spring of that year, a fire destroyed much of the forest on Newport's northeastern edge. When the fire finally burned-out, investigators entering the remains of the forest determined lightning initiated the disaster when a bolt struck a large tree. The tree that had been hit was, in fact, the large hollow tree located behind Bloody Tew's former residence.

Years passed; the burned-out forest gradually recovered. By 1886, young saplings were springing up from the ash and debris of the earlier burn, and wildlife was returning to the region. Peter McCallister was hunting in the rejuvenating forest in the fall of that year when the toe of his boot stubbed a heavy object buried in a soft pile of leaves. On investigation, McCallister found an oddly shaped mass. When he cleaned some of the dirt from it, he was startled to discover it was dozens of coins melted together; the coins appeared to be gold!

Carrying the hunk of metal to Newport, McCallister took it to Charles Smith's blacksmith shop. Smith, after examining the lump, agreed it had indeed been formed from the fusion of about two dozen gold coins.

When word of McCallister's discovery spread through Newport, residents flocked into the woods in the hope of finding more of the curious golden objects, but they found none. For months, the melted coins remained on display in a local bank, but in summer of 1887, the gold was removed and its subsequent whereabouts never determined.

In 1910, a Newport librarian was filing a collection of decades-old local newspapers donated by a resident, who found them in an attic trunk. Occasionally, she stopped to read articles and happened upon a report of McCallister's discovery. The librarian, aware of Bloody Tew's story and his lost cache, suspected a connection between the two events. After researching all of the available material on Bloody Tew, she arrived at an amazing conclusion.

The librarian suggested that pirate Tew had hidden his treasure in the hollow tree behind his house, retrieving a few gold coins each time he needed money for supplies. When lightning struck the tree in 1880 and the subsequent fire raged throughout the area, the cache of gold coins inside the tree was subjected to extremely high temperatures, and they melted and fused into irregularly shaped clumps. Given estimates of the large size of Tew's treasure, the librarian figured out that a great deal more of the gold was yet to be found around the remains of the old tree.

The librarian called a meeting of four close friends and described the results of her research. Together, they went into the woods to try and find some of the gold. Once there, however, they discovered that the ravages of the 1880 fire, along with thirty years of decomposition and new forest growth, eliminated all evidence of the old tree.

During the 1950s, workers cleared a wooded region on Newport's northwest edge to ready it for a subdivision. Throughout the area, roadways had already been created, and a few new houses were under construction. Just after a bulldozer cut through a swath of trees on one section of the subdivision, the foreman spotted a curiously shaped object sticking out of the freshly turned earth. It was approximately the size of a shoe, and, picking it up, the foreman was surprised at its great weight. On examining it closely, he was startled to discover the heavy mass was actually composed of dozens of gold coins melded together. One of the coins was of Spanish origin and dated 1690.

Newspapers picked up the story about the odd discovery, and several weeks later treasure hunters familiar with the Bloody Tew tale arrived in the area. Unfortunately for them, however, they arrived too late. The subdivision roads were already paved, and new homes constructed atop concrete foundations were completed on most of the lots.

Today, the remains of Bloody Tew's lost treasure lie buried under the manifestations of population growth and progress. It is very probable that the gold coins, melted together in irregular shapes, still rest only inches beneath the streets and lawns of this Newport neighborhood.

Pirate Collins and His Treasure Chest

Pulling the heavy wagon to a halt in front of the biggest hotel in Providence, the driver set the brake, stepped down, and examined the harnesses and fittings on the two horses. After making certain the animals were not badly chafed from the long journey from Massachusetts, he entered the wooden building.

Requesting a second-floor room overlooking the street, the newcomer paid for thirty days in advance and signed his name in the register—Peter Gifford. The desk clerk noted that Gifford carried two cap-and-ball pistols in a sash tied around his waist. The confident air of the stranger, along with the dark, almost evil, glint in his black eyes and the sinister-looking pencil-thin mustache, left the clerk no doubt that Gifford knew how to use them.

Gifford told the desk clerk he needed help carrying a heavy chest up to his room, and the man sent a small boy into the street to fetch two laborers. Five minutes later, the lad brought two men to Gifford at the wagon. After they introduced themselves as James Blake and Bernard Starkey, Gifford pulled back the canvas cover, pointed to a large wooden chest, and instructed the men to carry it upstairs to his room. With great difficulty, Blake and Starkey wrestled the chest from the wagon and toted it inside.

Pausing at the foot of the stairs, one of the laborers asked what was in the chest to make it so heavy. Gifford told him it was none of his concern and that the sooner it was delivered to his quarters, the better. For the next several minutes, the two men struggled step by step with the chest, finally getting it to the second floor. Moments later, it was dragged into Gifford's room.

The stranger handed each of the men a silver coin and dismissed them. Before leaving, Blake asked once again what was in the chest, but Gifford shooed them out of the door without answering.

After locking his room, Gifford drove the wagon to a nearby livery where he arranged for its storage and care for his horses.

With the first coin they had seen in over a week, Blake and Starkey decided to spend the evening in a nearby tavern quaffing ale. As the two men sat at a table in a dark corner at the rear of the pub, they discussed Gifford and the heavy chest.

The two men agreed that, judging by the heavy weight of the chest and the sound made by the contents as it was hauled up the stairs, it must contain a treasure in coins. Following their third ale, Blake and Starkey decided to break into the newcomer's room and see for themselves what the chest contained.

Blake and Starkey noted that Gifford left his room around dawn each morning and ate breakfast in a restaurant one block south of the hotel. Following breakfast, he went for a walk around the town, returning to his room at ten o'clock where he remained until sundown. Minutes after darkness fell, Gifford, wearing his pistols, left the hotel for the same restaurant where he ate a leisurely dinner and then adjourned to a tavern called the Bull and Bear where he remained until midnight.

The two schemers decided to break into Gifford's room one night just after he left for dinner.

During the second week of his stay in Providence, Gifford was enjoying dinner in the restaurant when he was approached by a burly man, red-faced with anger. The intruder pointed a finger at the diner and, in a voice loud enough for all to hear, accused him of being Peter Collins, the notorious pirate.

The intruder, whose name was McGinty, claimed he was a sailor on a ship that was attacked and pillaged by Collins who ordered his brigands to torture and kill all captives. McGinty stated that he was hanged from a yardarm but somehow survived. After he was cut down and thrown into the sea for dead, the pirates sailed away. Clutching a piece of timber, McGinty finally floated to shore three days later where he was eventually rescued by a British trading vessel.

Gifford sat quietly at his table during the tirade. After speaking, McGinty opened his collar and displayed to the nearby diners the mark of a noose on his neck.

Turning back to Gifford, McGinty told him he was going to kill him with his bare hands. Taking one step toward his intended victim, McGinty stopped suddenly when Gifford rose calmly from his chair, pulled his two pistols from his sash, and pointed them directly at the big man. A second later, the pistols boomed and McGinty fell dead with two holes one inch apart in the center of his chest.

After replacing powder and balls in the pistols, Gifford returned to his meal as restaurant employees dragged McGinty's body across the floor and out of the building.

For the next several days, whispers of what happened in the restaurant, as well as Gifford's alleged connection to piracy, spread throughout the town like a swift breeze. Some prominent Providence citizens now sought to join Gifford at dinner to discuss business propositions. Others avoided him entirely. Women appeared to be fascinated by the dashing and dapper gentleman, and Gifford was seldom without female companionship.

One evening during the third week of Gifford's stay in Providence, Blake and Starkey decided to make their move.

Huddled in the shadows of an adjacent building, the two men watched as Gifford ambled down the road toward the restaurant.

After allowing several minutes to pass, they crept into the alley behind the hotel and set fire to a pile of refuse. As the flames grew in intensity, they ran out into the street and, in loud voices, alerted those nearby of the fire. Peering into the hotel window, they watched as the desk clerk abandoned the front counter and raced out the back door and into the alley to fight the blaze. Once the clerk was gone, Blake and Starkey entered the front door of the hotel, raced up the stairs to the second floor, and burst through the locked door to Gifford's room.

There, lying near the bed, was the large wooden chest. Pulling a two-foot-long iron bar from his belt, Blake broke the metal hasp, flung the lid back, and the robbers leaned forward to peer at the contents. Hundreds of gold coins gleamed brightly in the moonlight that filtered through the window.

With what amounted to a quiet reverence, the two men sank to their knees beside the chest and plunged their hands into the rich contents. Swelling with the enthusiasm of their discovery, Blake and Starkey began pulling handfuls of coins from the chest and stuffing them into the pockets of their jackets and trousers. When they believed they couldn't carry any more, the two men rose and turned to leave only to find Gifford framed in the doorway, a pistol in each hand. Alerted by the activity generated by the fire, he had, moments earlier, raced back to the hotel.

Gifford ordered Blake and Starkey to empty the coins from their pockets and return them to the chest. When they had done so, he told the two men to pack up whatever belongings they possessed and leave Providence at once or he would kill them. The two frightened men promised to do so and slunk from the room.

As they were leaving the hotel, Blake forced a laugh and pulled a single gold coin from his pocket, telling Starkey he had held one back. Together, the two men walked to their favorite tavern, ordered ale for everyone, and told the story of the treasure chest in Gifford's hotel room.

The next morning, the town of Providence was abuzz with the events of the previous night. Gifford was soon aware of the talk, and decided he must leave as soon as possible before another attempt was made to steal his fortune.

Two days later, Gifford, his chest and other belongings loaded into the wagon, drove south out of Providence. That same afternoon, the bodies of Blake and Starkey were found on the shore of the nearby bay—both had been shot in the head.

Gifford traveled about ten miles south to Warwick Point where he eventually purchased a house. Here, attended by a manservant and cook, he lived a relatively quiet life. Occasionally he drove to Providence where he purchased supplies and books, but he never lingered, always returning to Warwick Point the same day.

During one visit to Providence about one year later, he was spotted by a Naval officer who recognized him as Peter Collins, a pirate wanted for a variety of crimes including murder, kidnapping, and robbery.

After watching Gifford drive away from town, the naval officer went to the local constable, reported his discovery, and informed him of the large reward offered for the pirate's capture. Together, the two men assembled a posse of some twenty men, and the next morning left for Warwick Point to arrest their quarry.

As the group of armed men rode up to the house, Gifford stepped out onto the front porch, a pistol in each hand. When the constable announced he was placing the former pirate under arrest and began to read the list of charges, Gifford shot him off his horse. The ball from the second pistol caught a posse member in the shoulder.

Throwing his guns to the ground, Gifford leaped from the porch and ran toward the woods. He was only a dozen yards from the safety of the trees when he was struck in the back and sent sprawling to the ground. Seconds later when the posse ringed the fallen man, Gifford tried to rise only to be gunned down once again, this time for good.

Returning to the house, law enforcement officers searched the premises for the chest of coins but found nothing. On querying the servant, they learned that, on moving to Warwick Point, Gifford hired two local men to excavate a hole somewhere on the property between the house and the shore of nearby Greenwich Bay. As the servant busied himself with household chores, he said, he watched as the two men dragged the chest into the woods.

The servant never saw the excavation and had no idea where it might be located. The two men were found dead one week after burying the chest, both shot in the head.

Though the posse searched Gifford's property for several days, no evidence of an excavation was discernible. Since the chest had been buried for more than a year, the site had probably grown over with vegetation.

To date, the Peter Collins treasure has never been found. The contents of the chest, believed to be gold coins, are estimated to be worth approximately $1 million.

Glossary

- **Bay:** A small body of water that serves as an inlet or an indentation into a coastline and is set apart from the main body of water, generally smaller than a gulf.

- **Boiler:** A part of a steam generator in which water is converted into pressurized steam and distributed to other working parts by means of metal tubes.

- **Boom:** A long, stout, rounded pole used to extend the bottom, or foot, of a sail.

- **Bootleg:** To manufacture, transport, or sell liquor illegally.

- **Bow:** The forward part of a ship.

- **Brig:** A cell on a ship used for temporary confinement.

- **Bullion:** Gold or silver formed into bars.

- **Cape:** A point or extension of land jutting into a body of water.

- **Confluence:** The point where two or more streams flow together.

- **Cutter:** A small armed boat in government service.

- **Deck:** A name given to a number of platforms on a ship that serve as a structural element as well as floors for various compartments.

- **Decomposition:** The decay or breakdown of organic material into simpler compounds.

- **Doubloon:** A Spanish coin originally issued in the seventeenth century.

- **Erosion:** The process of wearing away rock and soil by flowing water, wind, or glacial action.

- **Erratics:** Rocks and boulders of various sizes transported from their origin to a final resting place by glaciers.

- **Fathom:** A unit of length used, for the most part, for measuring the depth of water, though occasionally it was employed to estimate distances on land. Generally, a fathom equaled six feet.

- **Fault:** A fracture or break in the rock of the earth's crust, often accompanied by displacement.

- **Folded rock:** Layers of rock that have been bent and/or twisted as a result of compressional stress from tension in the crustal plates.

- **Gale:** A strong wind with speeds of up to sixty-three miles per hour.

- **Galleon:** A heavy square-rigged sailing ship, most commonly used by the Spanish for war or commerce between the fifteenth and eighteenth centuries.

- **Gneiss:** A metamorphic rock derived from granite.

- **Gunwale:** (Also gunnel). The upper edge of the side of a ship or boat. Derived from former use as a support for guns.

- **Hove to:** The past tense of heave-to, or to bring a ship to a stop.

- **Ingot:** A length of metal cast into a shape and size convenient for transportation.

- **Longboat:** The largest rowboat carried by a sailing vessel.

- **Man-o'-war:** A war ship, fitted with cannons.

- **Mast:** A long pole rising from the keel or deck of a ship used to support rigging.

- **Merchantman:** A trading vessel; a ship used in commerce.

- **Metamorphic rocks:** Existing rocks that underwent physical restructuring as a result of intense heat and/or pressure.

- **Moonshine:** Illegally manufactured corn whiskey.

- **Moonshiner:** A manufacturer and/or seller of moonshine whiskey.

- **Moraine:** A ridge or mound of glacial debris that was formed (deposited) during the melting phase of a glacier.

- **Outwash plain:** Plain formed in front of a receding glacier by the removal of material carried in the glacier by meltwater.

- **Paleozoic:** A geologic era extending from approximately 570 million years ago to 225 million years ago.

- **Piece of eight:** A Spanish coin worth eight *reales*. See *reale*.

- **Pleistocene:** A geological epoch of the Quaternary Age, corresponding to the Ice Age.

- **Precambrian:** A geologic era 570 million years old and older.

- **Privateer:** An armed private ship, generally commissioned to keep pirate vessels from attacking merchantmen. Term can also be used to refer to the captain or a member of the crew of such a vessel.

- **Prow:** The bow of a ship.

- **Rapids:** A portion of a river where the current is fast and sometimes dangerous.

- ***Reale:*** A monetary unit and coin of Spain and its possessions that is now obsolete.

- **Relief:** The vertical distance between the highest and lowest elevations in a given area.

- **Rigging:** Ropes, lines, and chains used aboard ship to work sails and support masts and spars.

- **Salvage:** Property or cargo retrieved from a sunken vessel.

- **Salvor:** One who retrieves cargo from a sunken ship.

- **Sandbar:** A ridge of sand built up by currents; generally found in rivers of coastal areas.

- **Scouring:** Refers to the erosive action of glaciers on exposed bedrock.

- **Side-wheeler:** A steamship having a paddle wheel located on each side.

- **Sloop:** A fore- and aft-rigged sailing vessel with one mast and a single headsail jib.

- **Smelt:** To melt ore; to separate it from the rock matrix.

- **Sovereign:** A coin issued by the United Kingdom containing one hundred and thirteen grams of gold.

- **Spar:** A long, rounded pole used to support a sail.

- **Spit:** An elongated extension of a beach into open water where the shoreline reaches a bay or bend; built and maintained by longshore drift.

- **Square rigger:** A sailing vessel in which the principal sails are extended on yards, or spars, centered and fastened horizontally to the masts.

- **Stern:** The hinder, or rear, part of a ship.

- **Stern-wheeler:** A steamship with a paddle wheel located at the stern, or rear, instead of on sides.

- **Stria:** (Striae, plural). Also striation. A groove eroded into bedrock by advancing glaciers; it may later fill with meltwater or runoff to form lakes.

- **Substrate:** Level of the ground below the topsoil.

- **Tectonic:** Pertaining to movement and deformation of the earth's crust.

- **Tory:** A name given to American citizens who sided with the British during the American Revolution.

- **Uplift:** Refers to portions or layers of rock that have been pushed upward as a result of compressional forces in the earth's crust.

- **Yard:** A long spar tapered toward the ends used to support and spread the head of a square sail.